Acknowle

Firstly, I would like to thank my mum and dad for always believing in me, no matter the dreams I have set. **I want to thank my Karl for always being beside me with unconditional love and allowing me to fill our entire home with my way to many books.** I would also like to thank Stuart Tricker for reading through the copies of my unfinished manuscripts and of course being one of my guinea-pig readers. Thank you to of course Joanna Minter for being the girl to give me the first book that started everything way back in high school. Like my mum has always said "Once you find your book genre, you will never stop reading" It only took her twenty years to find my dad's. I have to thank my cat Chester for always walking over my paper notes and laptop while I'm writing and a thank you to our new little pug daisy for taking all my attention so no writing can happen.

Lastly, I would like to say a big thank you to Meg Kearn for reading all I have ever written and thank you for always being there to give me a boost up. Thank you for editing all my work and I couldn't think of a better co-author for our book Queendom (to be released).

A fairy without Dust

A fairy is a creature, written in legend and sung in history but for me a fairy is a creature just like me. Small as daffodil and as quick as a dragonfly, fairies are not legends in my land. No here the legends of old are about humanoids. Here in my land, fairies are true living breathing things. How would I know this. I am one.

Do I have wings, yes. Moveable wings, definitely. Wings in fact that gleam lilac in the sunshine on the rare occasion I let them out, only shining when the light hits them. See through, they are, having been crafted from a membrane that I can place back onto my skin to hide if need be. According to my only friend Nerdiver, my lilac eyes glow when I'm angry, which has always surprised me since I have no dust to speak of.

Unlike the legends of old, fairy dust doesn't come from a tree; it comes from each individual fairy. Each bestowed with this gift, they can fly, bloom nature and pollinate the forest better than any bee. The lucky few can even connect with animals.

Me on the other hand, I am named Flighty. Somehow my mother couldn't have been crueller, seeing as I'm the first fairy in history to have been born with no dust at all. Long black hair just like my father, my parents don't visit often. With no need to spend time with their one son who cannot do anything like them, it's easier to just leave me to my life.

Even my so-called loving brothers and sisters, and there's ten of them, visit very rarely. Well, all except my youngest sister Spitfire.

The only one of my kind I can never seem to get away from is Psyc. The best flyer, bloomer and pollinator of my race, he always manages to pop up. Let's of course not forget he can speak with about every animal that flows through this forest of ours.

When I say ours, I obviously mean the forest is solely ruled by the elves, a kind race that pretty much leaves us fairies to our jobs.

What job do I have, well that's where I'm heading now. Walking, naturally, I am heading around a huge oak tree; though I find it much easier to climb over the outstretched roots, than walk the wide berth that they create. Taking the long route today, I want to do everything in my non existing power to avoid Psyc and his love squad of every other fairy possible.

Hopping up to the next root, the oak's roots are perfect for climbing with cracks in the stems, meaning I have perfect handholds. Reaching the top of the next root a gust of wind blows in my face, giving me a great feeling as it blows my shoulder length hair behind me. Scented with a touch of mint, I see the huge herb, crowded around the next baby tree, feeding whatever animal that may come this way.

Pushing through the herb next, I wade through some moss, spongy under my feet. I wear a fine pair of old brown leafed shoes that hug my feet warmly. Aged strongly, creating shoes from nature is one thing I can actually do as a fairy. Sun flashing through the leaves of a towering tree ahead, I begin to hear the noise of the up and coming river.

Running my hand next to me, I brush past a eucalyptus bush, flowering bright orange. Laughing at my own tiny size compared to the size of the flowers around me, I pass a cluster of bluebells, signalling that I'm getting closer to my work.

Bulked with muscle from building dam after dam along this river, I have managed to filter water into many different parts of the forest. Every place I've done this has bloomed better each year, my own version of helping the forest with dust. In fact, the only reason I started doing this was my friend Nerdiver. As a mermaid, you'd think she be in the open ocean, however, instead she comes to the surface of her small pond. With just enough room for her to swim around, whenever I visit we just moan about anything we feel like that day.

A big problem for me is always climbing up to my work of building the dams. Because I cannot fly, alternate routes are my only choice. Nearby the naturally made dirt wall that halts me from getting to my half-built dam, is a beautifully coloured green and yellow vine that grows up the side of a tall pine tree, with its roots growing right out into the water.

Jumping up I grab hold of the lowest leaf and pull myself up. Holding steady I jump up to the next leaf aiming mainly for the stems when I can. The strength of the leaves is fine but the steam makes it easier to lock my small grip on to.

Climbing higher than I need to, I can get a better look at what I still need to do. Re-directing the water was somehow the simple part, keeping a good flow to both the main river and my new stream is the hardest part.

Tall for a fairy, my bulk from running, walking and building every day has given me an unusual look for my kind. Most fairies are lean and sharp in the face. I, on the other hand, have had to remake every piece of my brown clothing to work around my big bulging muscles.

The last time my sister Spitfire visited, she couldn't understand how it was possible. For her my dustless-ness is no problem, she still loves me, but a fairy that can fly true, she will never truly understand being forced to do more physical things. When you're buzzing around the sky, never having to spend too much time on land, you will, of course, have the usual petite look of a fairy. Though a common trait in my siblings alone and Psyc of course, we are all of a taller generation to the rest of our kind.

Locking my mind on my main task for the day ahead, I push my side bag behind me, wedging it next to my pickaxe clasped to my waist. Aiming myself, I push off the vine leaf

I'm stood upon and grab the top of my new dam with both hands.

My skin having hardened from working with rocks so much, I've built this dam so nothing can knock it or dislodge the barriers I have created. Pulling myself up, I go straight to my pile of rocks, placed just outside my dam barrier. Lying in a wheelbarrow I made at the beginning of the year, it's made of the strongest wood I could find. Painting it lilac to match my colour was Spitfire's insistence, coming to my home while I was mid-construction. I would be lying if I didn't say I was pleased with the final look. Moving my materials to where I need them has become so much easier since I've had this wheeler, trying to lug them one at a time is far more time consuming.

With the sounds of the water pouring down the river into my new mechanisms, one wrong step and I would be off for a nice long swim. Doing it once or twice, I've learnt the best way to hold my body and step in the streams. Bending my knees to make sure I don't pull my back, I pick up a rock nearly the same size as me and manoeuvre it to my half-built dam.

Building for half the day, the sun has moved above my head, forcing me to put my hair up into a topknot to keep it out of my eyes. Sweat drenching my shirt, the sun seems to be on a mission to make me turn into water or to sweat my clothes off. Always wearing a similar style to the rest of the fairies, I am wearing a pale off-white cream shirt and dark brown three quarter length trousers.

Fitted to my strong muscular legs, movement is easy with the stretchy fabric. If I'm not building for the day, I will wear a colourful waistcoat, the majority of which are shades of greens or yellows. This style of clothing is perfect for flying in smooth clean air, but working with an axe or weight lifting, means sweat comes quickly.

Stomach grumbling I know it's long overdue that I had some food. Grabbing my small side bag which is a similar colour to the shade of my trousers, I hunt for a baby apple grown to the perfect size for a fairy. Being able to bloom plants and trees, ancient fairies found a way to grow miniature versions for us, the future generations. Though we mainly stick to our natural sources of food like seeds, my kind now bakes small items of bread and even fruit or vegetable pies.

Finishing off my apple, I look next for a pack of seeds that I have wrapped in a bright yellow maple leaf I get from the maple tree my home is built inside of. Munching quickly, my hunger has grown so fierce today. Taking off my top, I rewrap the food into my maple leaf and place it back into my bag.

Lying on the side of my dam, I ready myself for some sunrays. Closing my eyes, I love the feeling of the sun's kiss, the heat slightly cooking me, tanning my already naturally bronzed skin even more as I sink into my rest time.

Touching up my tan every day, my life is repetitive in some ways, which I like. Wake, wash and eat, I give my two floored home the small spruce it needs before I leave. Choosing to build as far out from the other fairies as I could, when I saw the sun touched maple tree and the bend in its trunk I knew it was where my house was meant to be. Building a terrace on one of its branches that comes out from my second floor; this is where I grow my own veg, fruit and seeds. Apples, I steal them from Spitfire's home like any good older brother would do.

Continuing my daily routine I walk to work where I build, eat, sunbathe, then I maybe round off my day with a visit to Nerdiver or I wander the forest for a bit. When you have a life with a rare amount of visitors, you get use to planning your day with ease. Other creatures that come into my life just disturb my peace really.

Sun easing off, I open my eyes hoping the clouds haven't started rolling in. Instead of the annoying balls of fluff, I'm expecting, I get the image of a shadow coming down upon me. Rolling on instinct, I move out the way, snatching my top, bag and axe in one quick movement.

Pelting for the cover of the tall grass and vines next to the river, I run, rather than try and find a pointless hiding place. From my own experience hiding, unless you bury yourself in the ground, will gain you a one-way ticket down a predator's throat.

Refusing to waste time on looking back, I stuff my shirt in my bag, as putting it on will have to wait. Getting away from a bird on the hunt for food always ruins my daily routine. My instincts working on overtime from years of what I have seen and had to do to escape, it does not mean I might not be eaten one day.

"Flighty! Wait!" A voice stops me dead.

Hearing nothing else I turn slowly, the only sound is the dirt under my feet. Seeing his cropped afro before taking him in, my disdain for the creature now standing in front of me, runs through me at the sound of his next words.

"Don't be afraid, it's only me. I'm not a bird." He says, seeming to try and calm me. Still breathing heavily, adrenaline buzzes through me, as I don't say anything in return.

"Sorry to scare you, I didn't think the way I was descending would make my shadow look like a predator" He says, giving me a godlike smile with his perfect mouth and his perfectly squared white teeth.

"You didn't think. Ha!" Turning about, aiming to leave the bane of my life, standing alone behind me.

"Wait. Flighty! I just wanted to say how amazing your dam looks. Actually, all your dams do. How have you worked out how to build them so well?" The perfect voice quizzes me.

"How could I possibly do anything as remarkable as this without dust is what you mean?" I huff, his breath-taking beauty already annoying me "Every time. Every time you come near me you always rub your amazingness in my face. I don't need your pretend pity!" I shout, picking up my pace to get as far away from him as I can.

"I didn't mean it like that. You're changing the forest, for the better" He says, sounding so genuine I pause.

"Where are your fans?" I ask, spinning back to him "Don't they usually follow you constantly? I didn't think you could even function without them." I ask, putting a bite on the questions, even though I didn't plan to.

Not following my march away from him, a big gap between us has grown. Following me while I have a two-year-old tantrum is clearly something he's not going to do. Clocking me eyeing him up, he pushes off the ground and fills the growing gap between us in one flap of his grand wings. Sun shining through the tall grass behind him, it glistens off the membrane his wings are made of, a golden hue running along the outer edge of them. His natural dust colour mapping the golden veins through is wings, he's doesn't understand how lucky he is that dust flows so freely for him.

Feeling my wings twinge slightly at the sight of his, I force mine to stay clasped to my skin. Curling over the tip of my shoulders, my lower two wings hugging at my waist. Tightening my control over my wings I do not want Psyc to see mine at all. Looking like a rather tiny version of the humanoids from legends, I roll my broad shoulders, trying to tell myself to relax around the best fairy in the whole forest.

Coal dark skin, Psyc's golden coloured eyes shine at me, giving off small amounts of dust from their sides as he looks at me. Even now the allure he is giving off helps me understand why so many of my kind are infatuated with this god. No matter how much I hate him, even I know a god in this world when I see it.

"What?" I ask

"You are quite a unique fairy aren't you Flighty" He smiles, pissing me off again.

"What is that supposed to mean. You never answered my question, where are all your followers?"

"I'm the fastest fairy in history. If I want some alone time, it's very easy to fly away. And I mean your muscles. You look like a humanoid of legend. Is it from not being able to fly?"

"Really?! You're so arrogant!" I spit, my saliva nearly bursting from my lips I'm so angry "You're the fastest flyer well, well done. I cannot help that I have no dust, but thanks again for the reminder." I seethe, his words ripping at my one true pain I always feel. "I'm so done with this conversation. I'm going and don't follow me!" Hating how he always has to rub it in my face how he never has to work hard for what he is. For me, nothing ever comes so easily.

"No, Flighty I didn't mean it in a bragging way" He begs, grabbing my wrist as I turn.

Reaching fast, I push him off, snatching my wrist away from his perfectly warm touch. Not meaning to push so hard, he falls back on his bum. Mixed with the feeling of regret and embarrassment for reacting way over the top, I cannot help liking the image of the great Psyc, the best fairy to ever exist being on the ground for once.

"Is that the colour your wings glisten?" He asks me, not fazed by my hard push or the dirt on his ass.

"Huh?" I reply, my flare of anger disappearing by his odd question and show of friendliness. Never having my wings out unless I'm home alone, I cannot comprehend how he can even tell what colour I have, he's not even this close to me.

Only ever visiting alone, it always feels as if he comes to annoy me. Brushing off the friendly manner he always has, I wait for his reply. Coming alone every time he pops up has always confused me. Never bringing a crowd, I can never think of a reason he wants to spend time with the one fairy without any dust.

Gaining no answer to my questioning, but instead an inquisitive stare at my body I say "My personal colour is none of your business, all mighty golden Psyc. The colour I am on the outside and in will never in our lifetime have anything to do with you" I huff, pulling my shirt out of my bag to put on, covering my wings entirely.

Getting to his feet, Psyc creates a small amount of golden dust in his hand. Giving off a serene glow just like the power in his eyes, his reaches into his pocket and pulls out a tiny fabric bag. Reflecting off his bright orange waistcoat, Psyc's white shirt and black trousers help his dust look even more godlike. Pouring his dust into the black velvet, he pulls on two copper shaded strings around the top, sealing the dust inside protectively.

"I have never come here to rub it in your face that you don't have dust. I swear I could not judge you on that fact. I just want to be your friend, a real friend. A true friend, anything compared to all my fake followers or fans, as you call them" He speaks holding out the cute bag for me, waiting for the acceptance of his gift.

"Is this some sort of joke? Are you just trying to make fun of me? The fairy with no dust. How sad he is, unable to fly. Unable to form any dust" I say sarcastically at first "How lonely he must be with no talent or magic to bloom or do even the simplest of things any of our race can do!" I scream making him take a step back. "Get out of my life Psyc! Leave me alone. Leave me to my non magical-ness!" I boom, somehow making some birds way above panic and flutter away.

"I do not need or want any pretend friends. You came here to brag to me, to rub your born gifts into my heart. Well, you're turning it black thanks to your little visits!" I shout.

Taken aback by my outburst, Psyc stumbles back. His eyes seeming to become a little wet as I spin him out of my sight.

"Just leave me be... please" I whisper.

"I'm sorry Flighty-" He begins. Moving away from him before he says another word, I storm into the waiting vines, leaving him behind.

Brushing past me so close I feel a buzz of heat where he touches me. My anger flares once again as Psyc nearly hits me. Flying up above me, a trail of his pristine dust comes off his feet as he flees to the crowd that awaits him.

How dare he! Is all I can think. How dare he come here and rub his dust in my face by pretending to give me some. That's a ritual only family or a true love can bestow upon each other. Who is he to offer me his dust, the best flyer, the best fairy for generations to come to this forest, to really pretend he wants to give me that gift. Maybe his fans have been watching all day, waiting for me to accept the dust, hoping it is for real to only get tricked at the last second.

Oh how I wish I could fly. How I wish I could show him. Show all the fairies who is the best, who truly deserves to be magical. Who deserves to make this forest bloom and grow into the magical place where creatures far and wide feel in their bones they need to come to the Elven forest.

Stamping on a twig the size of me, I strut away from my dam, my workday truly over with.

The mermaid of the pond

Nerdiver's water is unmoving, so still, it could be a rock. Huge granite rocks, big enough for Nerdiver to lie on if she wishes to sunbathe with me circle the rim of her pond. Created by nature or the elves that have trapped her here, the will of her masters shall always be a mystery. The pond is big enough for her to do a full lap if she wishes, the rocks circling the water fully, cage the water from any escape.

Behind the rocks is rim of grass area dotted with buttercups that have naturally bloomed. Guarding her world, trees taller than giants of the mountains stand strong, protecting Nerdiver's lonely paradise.

Using my self-built stairway, it zigzags in through the rocks centre, I go up to the highest one on which we mainly hang out on. Throwing off my bag I call out to my only friend, cupping my hands around my mouth. Taking me years, I have carved out the perfect caves angling so the sun lights my journey through them with natural brightness.

"Nerdiver!" I scream, the words reverberating over the water, creating a small ripple.

Still fuming about my visit from Psyc, I push my boiling anger down, waiting for Nerdiver so I can have my rant. Moving back over to my bag that is about to fall off the rocks edge, I pull out an orb of water I've collected while working on my dam. One of my secondary fairy talents I have managed to tap into is collecting orbs of water and hardening the skin until I need it. Why I can do certain tricks that my race can do, I am not sure. However, this talent is definitely one thing I am never going to complain about.

Sucking at the hardened outer shell, the water softens draining into my mouth. Easily hydrating me instantly, my natural reaction from a long walk and a fresh orb of water is a sigh in bliss. Creating orbs of any size, I usually carry five at a time, never knowing how long it will take me to get to a water source.

Calling out only once is all that is ever needed. Underwater and in the open air, Nerdiver's heightened hearing means she will always hear my call. The time frame of when she responds can vary quite a lot depending on what she is doing.

Running out from her trapped paradise, small tunnels allow her some adventure. However, they all lead back to here. Other openings into the forest were something the elves refused to give her. No escape, Nerdiver was placed into here as a tadpole and she will die here. Telling me the reason she was put here is something she refuses to do, though this cage of water is truly rare. Just like me, she is trapped in her destiny, unable to ever change it.

Refusing to let destiny decide our fate, I unclip my axe from my waistband and I climb over three of the huge rocks. Only ever being able to swim in the top of the pond, as I cannot breathe underwater, I know that if I cannot join Nerdiver, I will free her. My plan is something I have had in the works for years. Promising her on a day very different from today's sunshine, that I will build a new stream, one wide enough and strong enough to give my fin-tailed friend can escape.

Raising my pickaxe above my head, I slam down hard, chipping the crack I have formed along the outer edge of the rock, facing away from Nerdiver's pond. Connected to my crack on both sides are caves of stabs that Nerdiver has fashioned using her own dagger. As excited as me for her freedom, we spend the same amount of time, each trying to demolish these rocks.

Already digging a shallow route for the pond's water to fill when we break it free, it runs all the way to the main river that all my dams are connected to. Breaking these rocks is our last task to win this battle and I will win this battle.

The most annoying thing for Nerdiver has always been that she cannot survive on land. Breathing is fine, though she cannot change her tail into legs. Meaning manoeuvring the forest floor in a search for the ocean would be difficult.

Slamming again, I hit just right, breaking my small crack into a huge gap, ready to be pushed away. Walking along the rock edge, I move to a second crack, made from the new break.

Slamming hard again, my muscles shake as I hit true once more, snapping the rock in two. Always telling myself, just because I'm small, a task that is meant for a higher being is not impossible for me. Congratulating myself on this victory, I drop my axe, letting the clanging noise twinge up through me. Yellow on the handle, my pickaxe has seen me through many years of victory; its curved blade is something I give maintenance to weekly.

Sensing movement behind me, I spin, watching as the mermaid of the pond propels herself so fast out of the water, she can flip in mid-air. Before her snake green scaled skin sinks back underwater, I can see clearly how her scales mould into the smooth skin halfway up her bodice. Running all over her hands and up to her elbows, her scales match, turning into elven like skin as it comes up to her shoulders.

Laughing, I sit readying myself to watch the show she is going to put on for me.

Sailing back out of the water she spins on the spot, she throws her arms out as if she is a ballerina; the movement sending water in every direction missing me by an inch. Laughing along with me, her clear voice made by the almighty sings out. Lulling even my ears, her siren call can penetrate even the most hardened of ears.

Arms up, her cream underside and stomach draws my eyes as the sun reflects off her purple scales that for some reason only cover her breast area. Gifted by nature her full top half is of a woman, her chest forms the perfect shape of breasts that any elf or fairy would be jealous of. Her body curves in a way many humanoids of legends would have dreamed of.

Her tail, which is longer than her whole body, is thick, made perfectly for propelling herself under and out of the water. Green as I have said, her scales all flash the purple of her breasts when the light hits them. Asking if a mermaid's colours are unique like a fairy, Nerdiver told me once she cannot even remember the colour her parents were. Being given up at such a young age makes you want to forget them.

Head dropping back as she falls into the water again, she ends up upside down by the time she makes it back to the cold liquid. Hairless, her scalp has two holes in the side of it making up her deep inserted ears. Her heightened hearing comes from the complex map spread out inside them. Popping up the other side of the water, she winks her pure black eyes at me, no pupils that I can see whatsoever.

Tail moving underwater, she glides over to me, a bright smile spread all over her face as her sharp teeth, looking like spikes, bite together.

"Flighty" Her voice sings, washing over me, sending a need to jump into the water with her. "How's my favourite fairy?" Closing my eyes, I let her voice sink in as she has always told me to do. "I have missed you, It has been a whole week this time. I have a lot of moaning to do. But I guess you've been a busy bee socializing" She giggles, speaking just the right amount, for her natural spell to seep in.

Luring me to her pond accidentally when we were both younglings, she explained to me how she has a mermaid's voice, which calls out to anyone in the vicinity, whispering to their souls to jump into the water. Usually, in the ocean, this is the way sea creatures protect themselves and will lure in prey. Only here, it's how she gets her feed.

If mixed with a true intention of not wanting to bring you into her underwater world, a person a mermaid is speaking with can hold back long enough, that magical creature may push through her alluring spell.

Unfortunately for both of us, it always resets anew each time I return to visit.

"It has not been a week, I was here yesterday" I say through gritted teeth.

"Were you though? If only I could feel the days passing easier when I'm underwater" She says sarcastically "Unlike you, I cannot do so much, planning my day as you do is impossible. I do all my self-setting tasks too quickly"

"You will have to show me what goes on down there one day" I reply, my mind regaining full control. Getting to my feet, after realising I have fallen down fighting her call, I look up at my scaly friend as she pushes her arms up onto the rock I'm stood upon.

Her green scaled arms, standing out from the pink-grey granite her cage is made from, the stone makes a perfect pillow for her. Leaning her beautiful round shaped face on her rest place, she watches me, her eyes darting at the clothes I've sweated through today.

The same size as her hand, I walk over the huge break in the rock motioning at it. "Ta-dar" I wave, beaming at my success. "I need you to push the break apart, if you don't mind. And what do you mean you have nothing to do, you have your whole underwater garden to keep you busy"

"Did I say I haven't seen you for a week? This must have at least taken you that long. You're halfway through!" She gives a high pitched screech, getting over excited "I cannot garden every day. I need some other substance in my life. Now move closer to me and hold on if you need to" Unfolding her arms, I do as she says.

Nerdiver's serene smell fills my nose, dragging me back to her forearm for safety. Wet to the touch, her scales are both hard and soft at the same time, the sweet smell of her water lilies coming off her in waves.

Reaching past me on both sides with her hands, she grips the rock and pushes. Cracking loudly, the earth rumbles beneath me, falling away easily as the rock breaks so simply Nerdiver lands face first right by me. Knocking my bum with her nose she laughs, the excitement that her escape may actually happen sinking in.

"Sorry Fly, didn't mean to hit you" She says, not moving her face from the stone.

"Be careful lady. If you wanted to touch this bum, all you had to do was sing with force" I reply with a wink and a tap on my bum.

"Oh yeah, what about if I just poke it instead" She darts her finger out, tapping my bum again.

Laughing, the girl who always makes me relax and forget my anger and hurt I've felt all my life beams at me. Instantly remembering the reason I wanted to come here so bad, it bursts out of me.

"Oh! Psyc came on one of his 'rub it in' visits again."

"Really? Are you sure that's why he comes to visit you?" She says moving back into the water, giving me a look, trying to insinuate something.

"The thing is, this time he said all he wants is to be my friend. Don't keep giving me that look Nerv" I huff "He rubbed it in my face that he's everything I can never be. To top it off though, he offered me a bag of his dust!" Truly shocked by this, it reads all over her face how she was not expecting me to say that. Thinking for a second I've frozen my merfriend in place, I give her time to process it.

"He... did... not!"

"Did too, I swear, he even had the nerve to grow it in front of me first" I spit, my jealousy at his power shining through. "What an ass, trying to offer me the one thing I can never make on my own. You know, if it was the other way around I wouldn't be rubbing my greatness in his face"

"Maybe... well... if he said he wanted to be your friend, maybe that's a friendship offering because you don't have any dust? You never know, on the other hand I thought you said dust sharing is only for family and true loves." She says turning her head to the side, her insinuating look back on her face.

"It is. That's how fairies are made, remember. Two fairies combine their dust and form a youngling into the world. Though it only works if you have found your true love. He's probably given out his dust to every follower he has" Ignoring her meaning; I move over to sit on my bag for some comfort.

Watching Nerdiver as she slowly moves out into her pond, she moves her arms back and forth, stroking the liquid from above, then below.

"It's just, was he alone again? Funny how he has never comes down to see you when flying with the crowds" Nerdiver says arching her eyebrow or the curve above her eye anyway.

"It just makes me so angry! Why me, why can't they just leave me alone to my quiet life. I quite like it you know"

Hawking, a bird flies over; the only time I have no fear for them is when Nerdiver is with me. Yes, I am food to them, but they're food to her, so the risk of going for me isn't worth it when she can trap them in her voice.

"Ignore them. You are more special than any of those other fairies could ever be. Look at all the flowers blooming around my pond that you made grow" She motions to all the lavender coloured marginal plants and different waterlily varieties that fragrance her daily. "They need their dust to have a fraction of what you can produce without it."

"I just wish I…" Splatting down from the sky, the same bird hawks once more as its poop covers every inch of me.

Seeping into my clothes and hair, I feel the sloppy substance surround me. Making it to its directed target perfectly, the bird's poop sticks together.

"You have to be kidding me!" I shout, my day growing ever worse in every moment that goes by.

"Oh Flighty" Nerdiver's voice floats over to me "Hold still"

Opening my eyes, not being an option, I wait. Pouring out through her webbed hands, water washes down over me, wiping away as much of the bird's faeces as it can. Pulling my hair out from his ponytail, Nerdiver trickles more fresh water from above me, splashes it all over my face, cooling my anger as it does.

Leaving behind in its place, the sadness I cover up mixed with dread. Floating back to look at the damage still covering me, I give Nerdiver a sad twitch of my mouth.

"Take off your clothes Flighty; I need to wash them for you. Look at the bright side, your bag has somehow not been caught in the attack." Placing her hand on the rock next to me, she waits for me to strip.

"I'm not getting naked! I wear clothes for a reason" I inform her like she doesn't know.

"I am naked all the time, so do not pretend to be shy around me. I have known you way too long and seen everything on a few occasions so give me your clothes. I will tell you a tale that could be the answer to your needs."

Confused by what tale she would know that I have not heard from her before, I begin to strip. Yes, she has seen me nude when we were younglings, but many things have changed over time. Even though she may be one hundred times the size of me, it doesn't mean things haven't grown that she won't notice.

Giving in, I even place my shoes on her hand, followed by cupping my privates, I then wait. Bringing my clothes out to her, she brings her right hand over of the top of me again, pouring more water over me. Washing like I'm in the shower, I spin on the spot secretly liking this new way of pampering myself.

Feeling way more relaxed, comfortable and free just like when we were younglings, I unpeel my wings from my back to flap them a couple of times. Stretching my arms out, I sit on the edge of the rock, letting the sun, still in the sky dry me. Mentioning once again, as she always does, that she loves seeing the sun glisten my wings lilac, Nerdiver washes my clothes and begins her new tale.

Dipping my shoes one at a time first, she sings, and when I say sing. I mean she truly sings this time.

"Grown over time, thee tale for thee...

Of pure of heart can only see...

Thee well awaiting, to bless those willing...

For over time their lives have judged...

Them seeking of their rightful gifts... "

Washing my top she holds her voice, looking at me dead in the eyes.

"A lonely journey is ahead...

For any seeking that is lost...

Tests will hold your perilous way...

For thee who finds it will become...

Free from all that life has done."

Dipping my bottoms last, she stops singing to turn her head dead to me. Speaking five words into my soul, they secure my lonely path ahead.

"Thee Elven well of blessing"

Journey to a well

One sleep down and I'm already a day's march from my
treehouse. Map in hand, I drew it out onto the only thing
handy at the time, a leaf. My goal laid out ahead of me,
Nerdiver told me once she had sung her song the three tasks
set out as challenges. For a fairy with dust, these may not be
challenges but with me, they are pretty big ones.

Marked on my map clearly, I think I'm only a small stretch
away from my first one. The day of sunshine way behind me,
rain splashes down around me.

Flying in the rain, now that's a huge no-no. Getting hit by
droplet after droplets, mean a sudden push to the ground
can be deadly. Trying it once when she was a youngling,
Spitfire had a close call of nearly being skewered on a branch.
Getting your fairy wings wet is fine but if it wasn't for
Spitfire's now best friend Ellamight, who is an elf, my only
sister who likes me may not be alive.

The humidity of the forest has soaked my sage waistcoat
matched with cream three quarter length trousers and a
white shirt. Sweat seeping heavily out of me every second,
the rain helps in the world's task of drenching me. Glancing
at my bag I know my extra clothes will be soaked through
too.

Going out on a day of rain is dangerous for a fairy as it can
get big enough to knock me over. Droplet's the size of

marbles; the rain is thrown through the trees above, breaking apart until it hits through to the target, me.

With the raindrops falling around me, I stop dead at the sight of my first task. A high smooth wall, the size of the tallest tree in this forest, I have to lean backwards to see its peak. No grooves to put my hands and feet into, whoever built this wall must have carved it out of the earth. Pulling my axe out, I ready myself. Holding it firm before me, its sharpened point gleams ready to be used.

Digging in my bag for the two daggers that are ready to be attached to my feet, they clang as I pull them up, a string binding them together. Climbing up the stone, I need to hit the wall all the way up with force, to get to the top. Finding an alternative route around would take too long, with my tiny legs. Making it clear to myself why I am here once more, the usefulness of being able to just fly over this is clearly apparent.

Ready to go, daggers attached to my feet, I test my invention will work by kicking my left foot into the wall. Throwing my arms over my head, I put everything into hitting the wall, sinking my pickaxe in. Making a thunk noise, both pieces of metal slice into the hard skin easily. Made from a softer rock than the granite circling Nerdiver's pond, I feel my breathing cease as a raindrop hits me directly on the head.

Taking it one movement at a time, I take my axe in just my right hand away from the wall, filling the new hole with my left. Pulling up, I throw another swing into my axe, higher this time so I can climb faster. Sinking in, I bring my right foot up from the floor and kick with my knee bent up to my stomach. Pulling my left foot out, I hold steady with my axe as I bring my foot up to meet the right. Placing my empty hand just under where the slice made by my axe is, I pull the axe out, steadying myself again.

Swinging higher, I push up with both feet strengthening my legs, so I can get my axe up as high as I can. Grasping onto my axe for dear life, I put my left hand loose at my side now into the new hole, ready to repeat the movement with my feet.

Hitting the wall, again and again, I repeat this method all the way up. The sun ready to begin setting, I grow tired by the time I make it to the top. Pulling myself up and onto the wide carved top, someone has moulded this peak into smooth white stone. Brought up from deep in the ground, the colour of this rock has been touched by magic and then formed into creative slopes which I cannot see from here.

Next, to the wall is a high tree, with branches trailing down its whole body, waiting naturally for me on the opposite side to the wall I have just climbed. Breathing a heavy sigh, I grab a water orb from my bag and have a satisfying drink.

Rain ceasing while I climbed, all I hear is the patter of the rain dripping off the tops of the leaves all around me. The sound and small breeze I have always wanted to feel is clouded by finally being at this height. Seeing the view every other fairy has had over me, I understand the need to be in the sky as much as you can. The beauty from this high up is breath-taking.

Every little detail is unique, all joining together to form a glow of peaceful serenity. A serenity whispered by the creatures hiding in plain sight, the wall I am on holds back more wonders than the forest behind me. As if everything is on high alert, the ferns have wrinkled leaves rather than leaves that look like they have been cut. Bright green they sit about a huge bush I've never seen with off pale grey leaves, standing out from the tall grass before it.

No time to waste, I pull the daggers from my boots and reattach my axe to its place at my hip. Stepping back to the edge of the wall, I run and jump, propelling myself to the closest branch. Wings extending automatically, they flap, doing nothing to help me.

As they are made from membrane and I am a magical creature, when my wings unpeel from my body they phase through my clothing just like any other of my race. However, if I had dust in me, I would be soaring straight to the well.

Overdoing it, I land halfway down the branch, skidding to a stop at the centre of the trunk. Scraping my hands and legs, I ignore the pain, knowing there isn't much I can do to fix the grazes. Not thinking, so I don't talk myself out of this crazy plan, I descend out of the tree, into high uncut grass reaching for the sun.

Where I am exactly I'm not certain, knowing only that it's elven land. By the looks of this part of the land though, I doubt any elf has been here recently. Walking straight, I know my map said to head forward until I make it to a deer made of stone.

Where Nerdiver has got all this information I am not sure, but she must have more visitors than just me. I cannot have been the first creature to ever find her.

Noises to the left and right, the wildlife and magical creatures skulking around the forest floor, could easily find me. Holding my heart still, I wonder the way I'm meant to, not straying even for a glance at the life going on around.

A thump to the left, I look that way, only to see the spines of a hedgehog. Moving fast, something has the creature panic, my natural small instincts clicking in as I begin running the same direction.

Squawking from above, I hear a bird circling the grassland hunting for some dinner, the answer to why the hedgehog is running at all. Running on default, a ladybird bumps into my left, joining me on my new plan to escape the blazing eyesight of whatever bird is on the chase.

Making a funny noise, the ladybird eyes me too, wondering if I'm friend or foe. Eight black spots in total, it extends its wings, eyeing mine as I do same. Forgetting I have mine out, I give a small smile and a flap before retracting them back onto my skin. Moving on, I push my legs not wanting to give the predator a chance at an easy victory. Hearing it flap closer, I get pushed over by a gust of wind, brought by its feathered wings; my new ladybird companion is blown off into the green.

Dying as food for an animal, that can do the one thing I cannot to escape its hunger, would be the world showing it truly hates me. Beak coming down hard, the ladybird that has reappeared next to me, gets pecked up from the ground. In one second, it's gone, bad timing turning it slowly into food for the day.

Digging with my hands like a madman, I bury myself in dirt, hiding from the white dove that's come into view. Covering myself, in one last pile of dirt, I catch the gaze of Viking blue eyes shining out of the hedgehog I saw, aiming itself at the huge bird, its spikes ready to defend.

Closing my eyes, I feel the warmth of the earth, covering me, hugging my soul tight in its embrace. Hoping if I don't breathe, it won't know I'm here; I bite my lip and cross my fingers. Praying to the well of blessings, I hope the bird hasn't spotted me.

Stamping its claws on the ground hard, I hear the small battle between the brave blue-eyed hedgehog and the killer dove. Waiting for what feels like hours, the bird finally grows bored of its playfield, scaring off its opponent quite quickly. Quietening to a deathly silence I wait a while longer before feeling brave enough to crawl up from out the ground to see the damage. Except for a few patches, the grass around me is the only bit still standing tall. The sun vanishing completely while I was underground, I set up camp in my small circle of safety.

Eating quickly, I open my eyes from a sleep that feels like it went by in a flash. Bright for a morning, a glow coming from ahead of me is the thing I have been looking for next. Sitting up straight, the cream stone shaped as a deer, stretches tall off its block. No longer hidden by green, the overgrown grass here has been flattened all around me. A white clematis growing halfway up the statute, the green leaves let the cream stone get hit by the rising sun.

Checking out the deer, I see the elaborate carvings, edged into its skin. Covering everywhere but its face, swirls, odd signs and shapes glare at me, making me wish I knew the magical text only a few odd elves truly have power over.

Checking my map again for any risk of a misstep, I give myself a nod reading that I'm in the right place. Moving on, I ready myself for the second challenge.

Walking over to the nearest tree, I pull a fallen leaf off the ground and drag it over to the waiting riverside. Running next to the statue and off to another part of the wall that I climbed the day before, the stream is quiet in its continuous flow of water. Made into a minefield of antlers, the deer statue is missing all but one. Instead of being attached to where they should be, the antlers have been built into the long stream cutting me off from the well. If I squint, I'm certain I can see the pearly glow that is the shape of the structure ready to bless me.

Grabbing a stick next, I check my small boat will stay strong with its high curved sides. Pushing the orange leafed boat into the water, I jump in after it, making it bounce twice. Pulled instantly, the water rushes my boat, pulling me away from my true goal. Heading for the dip in the stream, the water funnels all the way to the white wall, a hole at the base of it, dipping down into hell below.

Pumping my overly grown muscles, I refuse to be pushed around by water that I usually re course on a daily basis. Once I get a rhythm, I turn my boat around, pushing all I have against the water. Screaming at the effort the water creates, I make it to the first antler, waiting for me to anchor to it. Similar to the statue, the antlers have long carvings running up them, embedding them with the same kind of power.

Moving on, I refuse to hit any antler with my axe until I feel too drained, knowing if I stop now I will not get this movement back. Passing two more, a gust of wind sends my leaf jumping in the air, spinning it, confusing my surroundings. Unhooking my axe, I hit out with the bent blade, ignoring the promise I just made. Hoping wherever I hit, I will be okay. Tensing my arm, I ready myself for a hard pull against my body.

Sinking into something tough, my boat drops from my feet; blown away by a second gust of wind. As if the wind is adamant I will not get to the well, I grip my axe handle, knowing my life depends on it. Hanging by both my arms already dead from rowing, I look down. Water streaming away, I've been blown up high into the antlers. High enough to feel every blow the wind sucks through this complicated bend of the bone I'm dug into. Surprised, yet I feel this antler is true bone and not stonework, meaning the ones of the statue where taken from a tree deer. Looking at my only route left to take, I gulp down fear that I may not make it to the end of this challenge.

Looking left I'm only two antler branches away from land, meaning the wind has surprisingly done me a favour. Apologising in my head for thinking the wind was against me, I thank it for getting me on the antler closest to the land I want to be on. Letting one of my hands go, I reach into my bag, going through it blind to find the daggers for my shoes.

Clasping one in my hand, I bring it out quickly and slam it into the bone above me. No feet this time, I stab and swing my axe over and over again, until I make my way up and over the first bend in the antler. All attached, I'm able to miss the second branch as I hover just above the water and aim for the last one.

My arms screaming in agony at hanging my body mid-air for so long, I do the only thing I can now. Honking up onto the top of the antler branches, I sit with my bum on the bones surface. Readying myself from a drop, I release the axe and dagger from sides of the bone, the only two things holding me in place. Sliding down and I mean fast, I arch perfectly over the bone's curved edge so I can go for land.

Propelled down the bend of the bone I feel each groove that the elves have carved into my slide, the patterns and signs I feel I should one day learn what they mean. Letting my instincts tap in I push off the antler as I make it near to the bottom. Throwing myself to the grass waiting to hug me deeply, I'm ready for its soft landing. Unlike the tree branch though, I do not make it far enough, missing the water's edge by an inch.

Forced into the water, I'm pushed along with the current throwing me into the bank further down the stream. Crying out, I hit instinctively with my axe. Somehow, luck is now on my side, I find a strong spot, enabling me to pull myself onto land.

Dragging my soaking self to the soft floor, I look up to the well. My final challenge sitting against the well's edge blending in with the pearly white stonework, begging me to try this last test.

Master

An elf. A fully-fledged hard as stone elf. Walking straight up to it, is brave enough. Climbing the ice cold creature is another thing entirely. From far off, I couldn't tell if it was alive. Seeing only four elves in my lifetime, I know their skin can look as hard as any rock, as it can be either crystal white, black as midnight or as bronze as a sandstorm.

Realising a foot away that it is dead, made my approach to its hardening skin smoother. Avoiding another onslaught of attack from a creature bigger than me is not what I need when I'm so close. So close to finally getting what I need, what I crave.

Arching my axe, I take aim hitting right where I need to. Thunk. Just like the sound that it made going into the rocks surrounding Nerdiver's pond over the years, this elf's skin is now granite. Hardening on the moment of death, elves like many magical creatures are gifted with immortal life. However this does not mean they cannot die, but when they do they turn to stone, or ash or even dust depending on the heart they possess. As the legends of old say.

Finding a journey up to the well's edge is my last task. Using this deceased creature will make it a little bit easier. Rather than climbing up the vertical bricks, this perfectly formed statue means I can walk up his long arm in one easy climb. An off-white, grey colour the elf blends perfectly with the overly expensive looking well bricks.

Wondering if your surroundings affect the substance you become when you die, I hope it is a long time until I have to find out. Fairies, unlike elves, usually have a long lifespan, but not an immortal one. A few I know to have existed, though I know of only one, who lives on the far outreaches of the forest. The one I have knowledge of being my grandmother.

Halfway up the serene statue, I see the blade pushed into his chest right where his heart would have been. A sly kill of surprise or a murder of passion, I see the reason of this elf who died here, killed with a blade twice the size of me. Leaning towards the latter for the reason he is at this well of blessing only, with a look of hurt on his face, it couldn't be anyone but a lover.

He either hurt another elf through breaking their heart or this elven man did something so terrible, a small blade to the heart, trapping him by this well is his lonely punishment. Metal and engraved with seven diamonds sparkling blue from the handle, an elf or dwarf took care crafting this item of death. All I can think is when I finally get to fly; the first thing I will do is break them out and gift them to Nerdiver for leading me here.

The hints she has given me, before sending me off to this journey, are carved onto my map, sunken into my soul for a lifetime memory. Life will make you climb as high as the sky, while water will drag you away before a test of courage will judge your soul. Making a choice, is your life more important than your missing part, will you drink from a well that could even be dark.

Making it very clear to me, Nerdiver said only the true and deserving will receive their blessing. If your intention is to cause harm, death will come swiftly and harshly. Think inside she told me, and dig deep into the small soul hidden behind my inability to not be able to create dust. She made it clear that I stand alone and see if my reasons for drinking this water coming before me, is worth the risk.

Knowing what having the gift that all my kind has would mean to me, Nerdiver sent me in the right direction, but making this choice is for me alone. Saying goodbye she said she hopes I will not do it unless I can be one hundred percent certain it will work. Losing me is something she could not bear.

Getting to the top of this well, I thought I was certain this must be for me. Gaining my power, by going through what I have to be here, climbing this story-less elf to stare down at this abyss.

This empty lightless cave, with no end in sight. Screaming at me, my wings want to flap away. A thick tangled rope runs down the centre of the well. Stretched black over the years of waiting for someone to use it, the rope hides the awaiting bucket deep in the wells bowels. Fallen away from me, my only way to get to what is beneath is to jump.

Making this decision alone, takes my mind back to my water friend. How lonely she will be, my only friend who helped me get this far is trapped in her cage. Trapped at the hands of a creature similar to the one behind me. Clearly not as serene and godlike as they make out, the elves of the forest have a twisted truth that the rest of my race does not want to open their eyes to.

Delving into my bag, I snag on the cup I brought. Bringing it out, I put down my bag and axe, crossing my legs as I fall to the ground. Placing my wooden cup in front of me, I'm unsure if I even need dust. I've made it to this well, all without the help of my wings or any magical dust. Why do I need a gift that didn't want to be a part of me to begin with.

Kicking out at the bright brown object before me, I watch as my cup tumbles the two bounces before slowly edging over the well's peak. Giving me time to reach out and grab it if I wanted, I let it go. My decision made at my core.

Waving goodbye, to the future prospect, to my most favourite cup I have ever made, I sigh a big breath of peace.

"Why did you do that little bug?" A voice sounding like two rocks scraping against each other, booms down over me.

Jumping forward, I roll, grabbing my axe and turn on the spot. Readying myself for a predator to get me, I give it a single heartbeat to check where the noise has come from.

"Boo" The voice blows at me, pushing me back into a crouch.

Attached to the voice is a rock troll, standing just above the height of the well. Face made of a flat oval, the rock is harsh, jagged and broken at points. Looking like someone has gone at his face with a blade, there is beauty placed onto him, with moss and orchids growing over his body and around his eyes. Big and round, his eyes are filled with black. His face made mainly of a nose stretching the sizes of his face and a thin line making up his mouth.

Placing his hands on either side of me, his round fists scrape at the stone beneath me, sending white sparks as he leans in. The moss covering the grey stone he's made of, his left cheek has the biggest cluster of pink orchids, growing up to meet his eyebrow that is a piece of rock rounding over his eyes.

"An armed little one aren't you." He smiles, nodding his head at my axe.

Raising it up, I say nothing; instead I just take in the solid being I've heard are dying out. Why he's even talking to me, or coming near me, I'm not sure. If jumping into the well behind me is my only chance for safety, my choice of not drinking the water will disappear quickly through no fault of my own.

"Not going to say anything? Come on little bug, give me something. Why did you kick that into the water? I know what this well is. Why are you in need of a blessing?"

"That's none of your business..." I say before I jump with my axe at his hand to the left. Slamming down as hard as I can, he moves his hand over, letting me sink my axe halfway into the stone of the well.

"Woah, careful there! I'm a friend."

"Rock trolls are no friends to fairies! You're nearly wiped out. I know of our race's history"

Taken aback by my harsh words, the troll seems to look sad for a minute. "Well that's not very nice, and in all honesty, I thought you were a pixie. Why haven't you flown away if you don't want to talk to me?"

"A pixie! Shows what you know. And again that's none of your business."

"Okay. Okay, calm down. You just seemed like you wanted someone to talk this through with. After losing your cup and making it all the way here, are you having second thoughts?" He asks, his voice scraping with every syllable.

"I've changed my mind. The elves can keep their blessings." I say, moving to return back to the elven rock leaning against this marvel of power beneath me.

"Wait. Please, why don't you want to talk? I thought fairies were meant to be friendly. How do you know that rock trolls are dying out?" He says coaxing me back.

"I'm not a typical fairy. I don't interact with my kind much. In fact, most are quite annoying. Overly peppy and happy with everything they can accomplish. Well, I'm different. And I have just realised I'm fine with that. I'm me and that is all I need to be. As for your kind, one of my sisters mentioned it once on her infrequent visits." I huff, relaxing as the words I say, I know I truly feel. "You must know fairy and rock troll history better than me. Rock trolls are immortal aren't they?"

"I'm not your typical rock troll either; I don't just lie at the top of a hill all day waiting for things to come to me. I make my own fate; I want to change the forest. I am my own master, and fate has no control over me. Rock trolls may be disappearing but that will change. I'm going to change it. You're going to help me" He demands, leaning back down to me, a smile on his hard face. "My kind use to be immortal until fairies and elves changed that. But I am not holding it against you"

"Me" I question confused by his speech "Why am I going to help you? You've done nothing for me and I don't even know who you are? How have fairies made rock trolls no longer immortal, stop lying!"

"I am no liar! The most I do is bend the truth or I choose not to speak it. Like you said I know our history better than your stories, though this can wait for another time." Taking a deep breath, he turns his long mouth into a wide smile once more "My name is Master. What is yours?"

"Flighty" I say easily, forgetting my anger at his brashness.

"Nice to officially meet you Flighty. Now, why are you at this well? What blessing do you need?"

"I… I have no dust. The first fairy in all of the forest to ever be born without any dust. Meaning I cannot do anything a true fairy can do. I cannot fly or bloom anything." I sigh, falling back down into a sitting position. Now I have finally told him, I'm not entirely sure why I was throwing shade at him.

"Your parents are very mean then aren't they" He states

"Huh?"

"Calling you Flighty, but creating a child who has no dust to be able to do the one thing his name says he is."

"Well I'm one of twelve, so I was forgotten quickly enough. How come your parents called you Master? That's an odd name?" I quiz

"Master is my own name. I have named myself anew, taking control of the life before me is my goal. My given name, I have left on the hill I was placed upon as a stone. My parents died on that hill, creating no more children, letting our race begin its journey to extinction."

"I think I like that. Not the extinction part" I say pushing my hands up at him, as his face becomes hurt "The taking control of your own fate, your own name. My friend Nerdiver had her own fate taken away from her from the moment she was a tadpole. Put into a pond by the elves for their own needs. If only I had to power to free her." I look up at the rock troll, who to me is a giant rock-god. "I'm trying, believe me, but it's slow going"

"So if you had dust, that's something you think you could change?" He prods, sinking slightly to come completely eye level to me. Not sure if his concern for her or me is real, I realise I don't care so much. Having an honest conversation with someone apart from Nerdiver is a nice change.

"It would give me so many more options than what I can do now. But she warned me not to drink unless I have pure intentions. I'm not one hundred percent sure I do"

"Nobody ever does little bug. If the intentions are there even a little bit, surely the risk is worth a try. If not, being trapped forever is worse for her." He says turning my ready-made mind around.

"If I die though, she will never be free. I cannot leave her alone forever"

"Okay listen, let's make a deal. I will give you a little of my power to mix with the blessing to help you gain whatever desire you wish to fulfil. I promise if my power doesn't help and you die, I will free your Nerdiver, however, you have to help me one day when I come asking for my favour in return"

Thinking inside, I cannot remember any stories of Rock trolls having any power. Made of rock obviously, travel in a blink of an eye I have heard and very durable, which isn't a surprise. Though a power they possess I have never heard of. Master is his name and maybe I need to trust someone else to gain the gift of dust. To save my mermaid friend.

"What power do rock trolls have?" I eye him.

"A rock troll's power is his own like dust is to a fairy. Asking me that question is too personal, but I will show you a tiny part now if you will agree to my terms. I will also need to know the whereabouts of your friend if I am to help her if you perish. Which is highly unlikely with the pure intentions you clearly have. Now little bug. No sorry Flighty. Will you agree?" He asks standing up straight and away from the well.

"One more question... how will you find me when you need the return for your help with this?"

"Again that is a secret only rock trolls are allowed to know. Do we have an agreement?"

Pondering for a moment more, I think of what it will be like. What I will be like when I have my dust. Will it be everything I wish it will be. Am I truly doing the right thing, taking his offered help. This risk is like walking into the mouth of a crocodile and waiting to see if it swallows me whole or lets me take the prize he has inside for free.

Nodding, Master claps his solid hands twice, his happiness shaking the well I stand upon.

A little troll help

"How am I going to drink from the well? I've kicked my cup away" I stare at the deep at the hole next to me, making a good point.

Reaching so far down, the water is nowhere in sight. Vanishing about a third of the way down darkness shrouds a bottomless well for all I know. Never thinking to ask how Nerdiver knew about the well, I must remember to ask her. Living alone in a pond with many tunnels but no other surface space, she must have more visitors than she's ever mentioned. Maybe the creatures that placed her there come back from time to time.

"No matter little bug. You could dive into the well itself, though I don't recommend it. I cannot gift you with some of my gift if you do. Allow me to create you a new cup." Master says his demanding stance disappearing with my mind fully on the water ahead of me.

"Master?"

"Yes..." He says, pausing from squishing his fists together.

"What about if it doesn't give me dust? What about if I gain a tail or something instead."

"Worrying about this now will not help you. And for one thing, I do not believe the blessing the well will gift you with will be a tail. You are a fairy. And fairies above all things should fly, so take a seat and allow me to work." He soothes my worries building inside as I sit with my legs dangling over the edge of the well.

The elven statue next to me, stares eyes frozen to look at the same show about to start before me. Still not sure what kind of power a rock troll possess, I wonder if they can grow items out of what they are. Anything else, I will want to know more about.

Pinching the moss covering his arm, Master pulls a small bunch off and places it into his left palm. Staring at the collection of moss, Master places his index finger at the top of his inner forearm. Looking to press hard, he scratches all the way down his arm, setting fiery sparks off, which take on a life of their own. Spinning around his arm, they aim for the moss, waiting patiently.

Making it to his wrist, Master then scratches around the moss, circling closer to the cluster of green glowing from the sparks diving into it. Tapping the moss on the top, he moves his hand away, letting his power do its work.

Rising up, the fiery glow envelopes the moss as it pinches up, moulding into a new form. Dulling, the moss has hardened into a snaked skinned stone, shaped just like a goblet for a higher being.

"A goblet feels appropriate for such risk-taking" Master says bringing the goblet over to me.

Climbing up onto his index finger, I take the goblet from his hand. Its weight in my hand, weights down my wrist. Flashing from the light in the sky, it seems to have small sparks swimming around the stone. Looking inside, the bottom is jet black, waiting for me to fill it with water to its neck. Eyeing it carefully, it's snake green skin, reminds me of Nerdiver, while it's touch confuses me, feeling as soft as moss, I know it is as firm as rock.

"Okay, let's do this" I say, nodding at Master to pull the bucket of water up.

Grabbing the rope, Master pulls hard, bringing up a pale white bucket attached to the rope. Placing it next to me, it looks to be ready to break apart, the wood cracking grey as it holds all the liquid in. Putting his hand next to the bucket, I climb back onto the rock trolls fist, allowing him to give me easy access to the liquid.

To what all of this has been about, all the fighting I have been doing my entire life. One of twelve, firstborn, the first one to be created, then to be tormented by my younger siblings for something I could never control. Today I take back the power; take the blessing, the gift I deserve.

Dipping my hand into the clear substance, the water fills my new cup quickly. Sloshing over my hands, the liquid doesn't look as if it is special at all. Looking like any other water flowing down the stream behind me, I look at my new friend made of solid rock.

"Don't falter now. You've come all this way, and I've done everything I can to help you. It's all on you now little bug." Master says, moving his hand back onto the well wall so I can get off him.

"Wish me luck?" I ask

"Always, and not just in this. If your dust is your blessing, I hope it brings you the joy you've always wanted." Sounding so kind and sincere, I bring the cup to my lips, taking one last breath in through my nose.

Downing my head back, the blessed water flows down my neck, knocking my body backwards at the sizzle it creates. Eyes closed, I feel the wall vanish beneath my feet as I drop backwards into the well. Screaming out, I view the world of light disappearing as I fall into the depths. Into the awaiting water I have just stolen from.

No help this time, I feel the water pumping into my body, taking over as I free fall into the unknown darkness around me. The prospect of death growing, my instincts take over as I unpeel my wings from my muscled body and flap them hard.

No response, the sizzle dies out as I push, willing all my fight inside to fly out. Float, flitter, soar, anything that a fairy with dust can do to get me to the sky waiting above. This is the blessing I want, I deserve. If you are going to bless a fairy that cannot fly, surely it will be with the dust it's missing.

Flapping a final time, the water flowing into my body makes a shift. A small shift, that if I wasn't aware of this free falling I wouldn't have noticed. But enough of a shift, I feel my first real flap of my wings that make a difference. Rather than dropping anymore or falling down into the water below that I will drown in, I hover. Bouncing up slightly, I feel my wings doing what they were grown for.

Shocked by the feeling I drop again, back into my free fall. Screaming at my own foolishness I pull myself together and flap again, harder this time. Feeling the air current knocking against the membrane of my wings, I push it back, lifting myself from the eternal darkness.

No sign of glowing, I bring the thought that my wings and eyes should be lighting up this darkened place and beat my wings again. Speeding the beating up, I manage to get into a rhythm, no longer falling with a bounce here or there.

Using my wings for what they are meant for, the air circles me like a friend that has missed me all its life. Hugging me closer, I stretch up, pushing myself to move to the free air. Wanting with everything inside my body to be out in the open sky, the blue world I have never been able to be part of calls to me.

Laughing aloud, my voice echoes around the well. Truly giddy inside, I cannot wait to see what Nerdiver or even the only sister I truly ever see Spitfire will make of this. My freedom from a trapped life placed on the ground as a Pixie. As a man who has to march to any destination he needs to get to.

Pushing up, I feel confidence in my new blessing to get me up into the world I deserve to be in. Laughing and whooping to myself, I hope to surprise Master, the troll who let me fall back into this well without trying to catch me.

His cup gone, falling much faster than me into the water below, will forever be bound to the well it was created to be drunk from. Growing lighter, I pick up my speed. The buzz of my wings flapping behind me pushes me out into the world of light once more.

Surprised how far I have fallen, I break the light of darkness and fly straight into the sun above. Reflecting off the metal ring wrapped around the wooden bucket, grasping to its old life, holding the water in; the light shines at me. Warming my body, from a chill I didn't realise I felt from the well, I flutter, letting my wings breathe the openness of this magical place. The forest I have dreamt of so many nights about flying above, to view the length and span of it.

Eyes closed, I spin on the spot, letting the conflicting air currents swim pass me, wishing to take me off into different parts of the forest. Waiting for Master to say something, I open my eyes to see the smile I know is stretching the whole of his face.

ᵔpty, the place where he was standing is no longer ᵔied. Turning on the spot, I check the whole circumference for him, thinking I may have come up on a different direction to the one I fell in on.

"Master?" I cry out, listening out for any reply. Floating back down to the well's edge again, I touch down. Heavier than intending my ankles scream with pain. Knowing its going to take some practice, to get the smooth landing like the ones Psyc can make.

Calling out once more, I mildly search for Master. "Are you here?"

Arching my view over the walls edge, I move around the wall, checking he hasn't sat down or fallen asleep, waiting for me to come back up. Feeling as if only minutes went by, I could have been falling and flapping for hours. Learning to fly from scratch takes time. Learning how to use this new blessing and what I have truly gained will take even longer, I am sure of it.

Definitely gone, I don't understand why Master would help me and then vanish. He didn't try to stop me from falling, but why then offer to help me. Not coming after me or even wait to see if I was okay, I wonder at this. Acting as if he for some reason cared for me, maybe he thought it didn't work and he had killed me instead.

Flapping my wings I push up off the ground, moving up and away from the well. If Master has gone, there isn't much reason for me to hang around. Just because this elf is dead, doesn't mean I need to wait for another one to show up.

Pulling my legs up behind me, I grab my bag while I lie like a plank. Laughing that I can do this with no effort, I place my bag over my head, letting it sit on the side of my right wing. Never having to usually worry about how my bag is going to sit with my wings pulled in, my new talent will change everything.

Hovering over my axe, I love the weightless feeling I get from using my wings. Dust sprinkling my feet, I don't look yet, wanting to save the view of the dust I have waited all my life for, for when I get to my goal. The goal is waiting for me above. Up and over the tree line, I want to see my lilac dust as I see the green land I am part of.

Not clipping my axe back onto my side, I push off over to the eleven statue, remembering to get my present for Nerdiver. Flapping too vigorously, I whiz past my aimed goal, the diamonds in the blade silently laughing at me.

No longer feeling the anger that used to burst with everything that went wrong in my life, I re-direct myself and push towards the blade again. Hitting my target perfectly, I slam my body into the blade, holding on for dear life as my wings don't respond as I want them to. Practise makes perfect, and with all the dams I've built, I know that this is how anything in life you do will finally work.

Seven in total, the diamonds circle the end of the silver blade. One big diamond set in the centre while the rest are set around it. Half hovering and half balanced on the top of the blade, I quickly go through my bag throwing out anything I have no use for. My trusty shoe daggers I drop, letting them clank against the statue as they fall. Pulling out an orb of water, I drink it up, letting the fresh water of one of my streams wash away the metallic bitterness the well water has.

Nibbling on some seeds, I drop the rest of the contents out onto the statue again. My need for a tent gone, I let all my camping items free as well. Tonight I will be back in my little home, my new talent of flying, meaning I can cross distances faster than I ever could before.

With an empty bag ready to fill with diamonds, I swing my axe, with a familiar movement I'm use to. Missing my first swing, I practise a few more times, getting use to the movement of having to hover still while swinging off balance. Hitting true on my seventh hit, I pop the first diamond out with ease. It falls into my waiting hand; the size of the diamond is the same as my chest. The hefty weight would be no match for a usual fairy, but I, on the other hand, move it easily into my waiting bag.

Doing the same to the other five diamonds dotted around the blade, my bag slowly gains weight as I drop them in one at a time. Heavy, but not so heavy I feel a difference in my flight, I go for the last diamond.

Sized the same as my whole upper body, I'm not sure if it will fit in my already overflowing bag. Looking behind me, I see on the floor, a pile of rope that I dropped while emptying my bag. Flying down, I collect it, bringing it straight back up to the last piece of my prize for Nerdiver.

Tying the rope around myself, I create a holder for the diamond to slip into on my front. Hitting my axe at the diamond, I feel the first sign of sweat I've felt since beginning. Hitting the blue sparkle at four points with the blade, the handle has slowly lost its beauty thanks to me. Finally wedging the stone out, I let it fall into the newly fashioned holder. Tying the top of the rope I left loose, I manoeuvre it up and around my neck for support. Bouncing a few times to see if any of it's loose, the weight on my body and neck is durable.

Holding back onto the end of the blade, I smile to myself. Not only will Nerdiver be getting to see my true blessing thanks to her, I have the best gift to give her as a thank you.

Certain I will never find out what this elf did to deserve being stabbed, I whisper a thank you to the vanished Master, for without his push to get me to drink the water, I would never be doing this right now.

Aiming high, I shoot off like a little bolt, finally fulfilling my goal to see the open sky.

The consequence

Varying frequently, stretching as far as my eyes can see, trees run off all around me. Patches of green, the top of the forest is dotted with sprinkles of auburn, the autumn begging it's descent upon us.

The forest looks as if the elves have laced difference in the types of trees together, so any onlooker would wonder who planted this forest, letting the variety pop up where they want. Rather than a typical forest full of pines or a sea of oaks brushing each other, my forest is truly where nature is in control.

Looking just as I imagined, the top leaves clash with the blue sky above, fighting each other for the sun's light kiss.

Wanting to keep flying higher, my new goal is to move beyond this height and go within the clouds. All fluffy and cute, they appear every few minutes, waving at me as they are blown by. With the wind touching their sides, the clouds are shaded cream and grey making shapes where there shouldn't be. If it wasn't for Nerdiver's gifts holding me back, I would push myself on. Fly so high, all I want is to become a god, journeying to sit on a heavenly throne.

Hovering in the same spot for what, I'm certain is nearly an hour; I still do not want to move on. Even with my new weight pulling down on my body, the diamonds continuously try to signal to me that I should get moving. If I don't leave soon, being able to get back home will never happen.

Forcing myself to think I haven't travelled all this way, tested myself and risked my life with a simple drink to end up dying from a fall of this height. I know may be able to hold this weight now, but flying the long distance home will surely take its toll. Pulling on my soul, leaving this view and moving on with my new life still, I can feel an earthquake of nervousness inside of me.

Surveying the scene one final time, I hold out for another long moment, berating myself into descending back down to the treeline below. Flying true, I know this feeling will never get old.

The smile Spitfire or even Psyc gives whenever they use their wings is something I could now understand. A feeling of achievement, freedom buzzing through me, I cannot wait to show my little sister the dust finally flowing through me. With the right part of me she always wanted me to have; now intact I know she will screech with joy.

Now I'm able to move with such weightlessness, we can finally do it together. In fact, when she was a youngling, Spitfire first refused to fly, stating it unfair that if I couldn't join her, she would not soar the heavens.

How I almost didn't drink that water, how I almost never let myself feel this pure, this magical. I will never let myself forget the gift I nearly threw away.

My thoughts quickly flashing to the rock troll that helped me, I cannot help but think if only Master was around so I can show him my new found boundlessness. With the ground under the empty air beneath me, I am certainly no pixie now.

Floating back down slowly I manoeuvre myself over to the wall area, giving my once in a lifetime quest a last glance before I fly on. The white bricked well, with the frozen in time elf, winks at me as the sun catches the side of the metal ring still holding tight to the bucket. Antlers still protruding from the stream, I give a quick dash through them, laughing at the ease this quest would have been if I had had wings all along.

Giving one final look at the overgrown flowers circling the deer statue, I wonder if I should find a way to return one day to take a cup of the well of blessing's water to Nerdiver. Maybe her blessing will be the freedom from her pond she has always wanted. Taking note of my own idea, I fly towards the wall I climbed only the day before.

Buzzing closer to it than I need to, I see the carved marking covering the deer statue are also all over the top of the wall. Designed to represent waves, the mould I climbed is clear now, the carvings all over them warding off evil from this place. Moving to the base, I want to rub my hand the whole way up the stone, flying to my awaiting future with a last touch of blessings.

Getting home far quicker than I thought I would, I burst through my door, hidden at the back of the base of my maple tree. Using glass or bright flower petals, other fairies make their homes as welcoming as they can. Me on the other hand, I have blended it into the bark as best I can. Having to usually walk all the way to the top of my tree using the interior stairs I cut out by hand, I thought it only right I do the same now. Just because I can fly, doesn't mean I want to lose my muscle bulk by using my terrace entrance.

Wanting to drop my newly acquired weight, far quicker now I'm now back on my feet, I power through the steps. Winding up in a tight circle as they rise, the steps follow the right bend in which the tree has made when growing. Placing all Nerdiver's diamonds on my workbench, I drop onto my bed, sleep calling to take my mind right away.

The last thought I get, flashing through my mind as the setting sun streams through my huge bay windows that look out on my beautiful terrace, I cannot help feeling happy I'm home.

The last rays of light reflecting off the biggest diamond next to me, I wonder how will I begin to create my dust from scratch. Learning to fly was on instinct, creating my dust will be something completely different I imagine. With the colour lilac swimming in my head, the day's journey leans on me to pass out.

F

Kicked awake, I jump out my skin thinking I will see another fairy before me. Movement no, sound no, instead my room is silent and no one is in sight. My empty home shining its warmth, the light brown wooden interior calls for me to relax. Moving from my leaf formed bed, I created using the leaves attached to the tree I'm inside, I skulk around my home for a culprit.

First checking my upstairs, here I have my bed with a built-in walk-in wardrobe attached on the left. To the right, I have my workbench and station, taking up most of my upstairs floor, as working into the night is common. Needing quick access to the soft comfort of my pillows it felt like a no-brainer I put it all on the same floor. Empty, I check the room I carved out of the bark into a washroom. Filtering rainwater down into a constant fresh pool of water, there is a small gap where a second branch on the outside helps direct the rain into the room, catching any droplets of water aiming to fall straight to the floor.

A dead end on the culprit, I walk over to my bannister, looking over the edge at the first floor below. Empty once again from movement and sound; I look up at my terrace. With open air between us, the terrace has the same amount of space that my bedroom makes up between us, hiding any culprit it wants. Eyeing the outside world through the glass, I can only see my vegetable and fruits, all ready to be picked and eaten.

Designed so my kitchen, lounge and relaxation area have no windows in, I wanted the light to solely come from the bay windows above. With separate stairs growing up either side of my home; I purposely can only get to my terrace if I first descend to my lounge.

Finding nothing, I walk over to the bowl of water next to my bed, rubbing my face in it as it goes a dark brown colour. With a fresh splash, I bring the coldness I need to feel to give myself the push to venture into my washroom for a real clean. Bathed and fresh smelling, I put on some new clothes. Deep mustard gold, I wear one of my favourite coloured waistcoats, wanting it to match perfectly with the lilac of my soon to be seen dust. With a cream shirt on to complement my colour choice, I feel every bit the newly powered fairy I should feel.

Ready more than anything to find out how to form my dust, a much-needed date with my half made dam is needed. Knowing that where I work the most, is the place where I will find my power. Leaving my home the traditional way I promised I would, I squeal like a small youngling ready to find out what I have building inside me.

Flapping lightly, I still feel the dust sprinkling on my feet, dusting me from behind with my power. Flying as easily as I am, I can't wait for my dream to end and for me to wake up next to Nerdiver on one of our sunbathing afternoons.

Still not wanting to see my own dust in case it is all a lie I have imagined, I half pretend that the first time I see my dust; I want it to be growing in a pile in my hands. Seeing the winding way I usually walk, I follow the path my old route goes. Dipping down to hover just a pinch away from the ground, I scrape my fingers on the dry dirt below.

Still wanting to practice all I can, I move in ways I should never need to make. Wanting to be the best fairy I can be, I know I can be better than that fairy Psyc will truly ever be.

Watching the earth as I whiz by, I let my eyes glaze over, not letting them be torn away by anything coming out of the ground. Well until… a tiny black bag flashes by my sight. Stopping dead, I spin pushing myself instinctively back to the bag.

Getting closer, I see the familiar item, something I was nearly given a few days ago. Tied together perfectly, I see the velvet shiny fabric, calling out for me to take. It's golden string calling out to me, wanting me to use it, for when the time comes when I need it.

Snatching out, I refuse to let my jealousy and old anger still control my life. I may never need to use Psyc's dust; but I tie it onto my belt, knowing only a fool rejects someone else's dust twice, when it's obvious the forest wants you to have it. Until I can work out how to get my new blessing to work fully, I shall keep this close, as a comfort, I would never admit to needing.

Planting my feet on the ground, I pull my wings back onto my skin, letting them rest from my over usage. Excited to finally have them working, I walk towards my lonely dam. Hearing the usual forest noises in my ears, I close my eyes and take a deep breath, taking in the freshly bloomed dahlias.

In through my nose, I count to one before releasing a long blow of wind, to the grass around me. Taller than I am, I stretch my left arm out at the fine green stems growing everywhere. As my finger touches the grass, I can help but want my dust to flare into action and grow these stems even more.

Hands back to me, I cup them together. Feeling as if this is the moment. This moment before I create, is the moment I need to call my dust to come to me. To fill and grow, so it can sparkle in my palms.

Doing as I ask, I feel a swell, a wave coming up through my hands and up into the open world. Breaking through the barrier of my hands, my dust surfaces, bowling into the cup my hands have formed for it. To do with it I am not sure, but the colour and look make me pause.

Starting out the lilac of my eyes, it is quickly overshadowed, turning into a dark black, where no glow comes from it. Heavy as a cold mound of death, my dust feels wrong, calling out to the part of me I never knew hid there.

The colour of a fairies dust matters greatly to them. It is the light of their lives, the sparkles of the forest, but it is something fairies have never been able to control. With a slight glow for some, others have dust that sparkles like the sun. Even if it's the colour of midnight black, it is pulled from the night sky and dazzles any who will get to see it.

Mine, on the other hand, feels like it wants to snake out of my hands, run into the woods and form a darkness no one is allowed to escape from. Dread filling me, I break my hand apart, my dust raining to the ground in a pour of hatred.

Hatred for me, hatred for Psyc, hatred for my mother and my father, but most of all hatred for the rock troll that made me drink that water. The blessing of an elf I was meant to get, but instead, I have wound up with a trick of a rock troll, and somehow a friend I trusted the most. Did Nerdiver know there would be a consequence to my blessing, did she know this could have happened to me.

Sinking into the brown dirt at my feet, the floor seems to rot on the spot. Turning into a hole of grey ash, it dies because of me. Because of my selfish need to be able to do this, to grow the one thing a fairy needs to bloom the forest. But not kill it.

Thinking I had stopped producing more dust when I broke my palms apart, I notice that dust is still sprinkling out of me. Spurred on by the anger I thought I had ridden myself of, the anger that has given me the push to do everything I have achieved over these years. I feel a panic, knowing now my anger is rooted so deep, I may never stop.

Spreading like a wildfire, my dust sprinkles onto the grass stems around me, the fool in me thinking if I flap my hands the dust will stop. It has to stop, I cannot single handily kill this forest, kill my home.

Breathing way to fast, I feel my heart bursting, the dread of pain I feel inside wanting to rip its way out. Circling down around me, my new found gift does the exact opposite to what I have always wanted. Blistering everything as I scream, I scream to the sky above. To the new friend I have fooled myself into believing was the answer to all my problems. Instead, an arms width around me it is taking the life force from everything in my small vicinity.

Snatching both my hands under my armpits, I drop onto the floor with my head on my chest and my legs crossed over. Leaning forward, I circle in on myself hoping this trap will take my dust away from me.

Terrified to move I stay frozen in place, twitching as I feel my dust continuously breaking through my golden skin. My dust hoping to breathe the still air of death, I scream, my vocal cords being the only thing I allow to move. Scratching down my clothes, it thinly rips into the fabric, changing my small amount of knowledge on dust completely around.

"Why me!" I cannot help but scream out at the world, as the shadow of death closes over me.

Feeling the pressure of something on coming, I decide I'm in no mood to hide or cower. Throwing my right hand into the air I look up at the last minute, gaining the view of a bird getting a layer of dust all over its wingspan. Screeching as my dust hits it, the bird that's been hunting me for months tries to flap away. Instead, its wings blast my dark dust all over the greenland underneath, its darkening body disappearing out of sight. My dust burning at the life force that it's snuffing out, it crawls as far as it can, getting to as much of the forest before something good may step in.

My vision drawn once again to my enemy, the bird re-appears squawking away as it leaves a trail of blistering feathers behind, my dust stopping its destruction and reach to everywhere instantly the bird flees. Switching into the correct mind frame, my new defensive power pings an idea in my head.

What if this dark dust is needed in the forest. What if it's needed to keep danger away for the smaller race of people. A race of people who apart from bees keep this forest blooming full of life, of safety. Maybe a blessing is made, based upon what the world really needs. Even if the drinker doesn't know what needs to be done.

A consequence this is, however, a curse... maybe not. Blessing or a curse, whatever the well grants, a consequence must be given. Though maybe my curse could be the real blessing for all fairies, even Psyc.

Unnecessary revenge

Changing my mind, I'm sure I want to create Nerdiver's present before I see her. Turing up empty-handed, I feel cannot happen. Finding a few sticks or a branch small enough for me to carry is what I need. Just giving the diamonds as they are to Nerdiver is not an option. My plan, I think, is to form a tiara, as it is something she can always wear. Gifting her with the headpiece of only royals is the perfect way to say thank you.

Brushing off the new information about my dark dust, I have turned away from Nerdiver's pond, heading to another part of the forest to find what I need. Populated by many more fairies than the parts I usually visit, I know for sure that they will not be around. With the sun as high as it is and the blue cleaning out any greyness in the sky, the fairies will be at the Suntime celebrations.

Partying whenever the world is like this, it was always another thing I could never be a part of. Suntime celebrations take place at the top of an ancient eucalyptus tree, so tall it stands five times taller than any other tree in the forest. Feeding the tree with all their dust at sunset, the tree has become the most powerful beacon of fairy power in the woods.

With my whole entire race distracted it means this is the perfect time to hunt for the materials I need. Flying past a cluster of tree homes, I catch a glimpse of something shiny. Stopping, I hover, descending slightly to catch a better look.

Planted by fairies so long ago, the fairy homes before me all look onto a courtyard in front of each other. Seven trees in the centre, they all have bloomed into thick-trunked giants so at least seven fairy families can all have homes in one tree alone. With ten courtyards like this dotting around this part of the forest, fairies populate a giant amount of the woods. Having colonies everywhere they can, we even have one in the heart of the elven city.

I am truly the first fairy to ever live apart from a colony, well except my immortal grandmother. With their colourful petalled doors running up the sides of the trees and windows and terraces bringing bright light to the interiors, my sight can only be drawn to the single home built apart. Small and quaint, whoever lives here must be loved by all. Choosing to live in such a small home means they also must enjoy their peaceful alone time.

Pale cream in colour, the fairies house is a closed up flower. Three times the size of a normal flower, it has to have been grown into this placement, by a gifted one of my race.

Standing alone at the base of one of the seven trees, the gigantic oak tree looks down warmly, protecting the creation at its roots. Piled up outside it is a pile of metal rods. Where they've come from or how they got here, I do not know. Fairies usually aren't known for creating metal things themselves, but I haven't been to a colony in years, a lot could have changed. Perfect for my tiara, I think I'm about to become a thief.

Whistling out, I wait.

I wait for anyone who didn't want to go or couldn't leave their homes for the Suntime Celebrations. With no reaction, I drop down, much smoother than the first time I ended a flight. Giving myself one last chance to not do this, I counter myself that this is for something important. Finding these big pieces of metal is a miracle. Unless with my time away from the main hub; fairies truly have someone who has worked out how to become a blacksmith, just like the dwarfs.

"Hello!" I shout as loud as I can "Is there anyone in real need of these metal rods? I'll take them unless someone talks to me in the next five minutes" I say, giving the non-existent people time to stop me.

Trying my best to be an honest thief I lean on the wheel barrel my soon to be poles are in and I wait. Using my time wisely, I try and think about anything else my new dust can do. Maybe it wasn't a curse or a fault in the blessing, maybe a gift I was meant to have. Letting my power loose though when I'm completely new and un-practised would be a catastrophe. Destroying all these fairy houses is not the way I wished to gain control over my dust.

With no answer to my request, I give a nod thanking the light petalled home and turn the barrel in the direction of my home. Living as far enough away from the rest of the fairies as I could, my sister wouldn't let me go as far as I really wanted. Finding a plot for me to live alone, Spitfire was very particular on how far from her colony of trees it could be. Near enough that she can fly and see me within an hour's flight, means my walk from here with this barrel, will take me at least half a day.

Walking as fast as I can, I don't dare use some of my dust to try and make the barrel float. Not even sure if my black dust can do that, I know I need to find a safe place to practise this new kind of magic I have.

Bending around a tree root, I leave the villages behind, knowing no one will know it was me who has taken these rods. No one will even suspect I could be the culprit of this theft, most of my kind don't even remember I exist. If only Psyc could be a mildly bad guy, then they may blame it on him. Knowing deep down my hatred for him is solely based on what I could never do until now, I let the thoughts of him sink out of my head.

Drawing my eyes to the left, a flickering image buzzes up to the tree line. Recognising that golden trail dust anywhere, I know instantly that it's Psyc, clearly on the hunt for something. Positive I shouldn't, I unpeel my wings and lift of the ground, leaving the new barrel behind.

If I give him just a tiny little scare, that wouldn't be so bad. It's only a little bit of fun, just a small bit of payback. Aiming directly for him, I don't hold back on the new speed I have gained flying as much as I have. Shooting for the kill, I wait to make a noise, timing it so I can be right on his tail. Rotating up so I am above him, the sun reflects perfectly off his huge golden wings, shining so brightly he could be a drop of sunlight.

A wings breathe away, I scream at the top of my lungs, scaring myself a little with how loud I am.

Dropping from the air so suddenly, I panic hoping I haven't just made him have a heart attack or faint. Following him down, I drop letting myself free fall, gaining speed on him once again. Never looking back, Psyc seems to ignore me more than anything, not wanting to interact with whoever is behind him. Angered by his ease of a reaction, I give chase, needing something considerably more to smooth my jealousy out.

Watching him as I fall, I see the ease of his head go rigid. Following his sight, I clock the barrel, patiently waiting for me to take it home. Flapping his wings again, Psyc flutters down in one final swoop ending at the opposite end of the barrel. Catching each other's eyes, I still hover as he really looks at me for the first time.

Touching one of my acquired rods as I move in closer, his eyes bulge at seeing me mid-flight. Angered by his hand on my prize, I forget that I stole them in the first place. Aiming my stupidity at wanting to scare him off, knowing inside I cannot lose my rods, I let my mind loose.

My instincts taking over, they are mixed with my building jealousy. Throwing a sprinkle of my dust at him, it lands as hard as I do.

"Get away from my rods!" I shout, my hatred clear.

Taken aback, Psyc drops to one knee, my dust blown over to him covering his wings, tinting them black. Unsure what my dust will do to him, I drop to his side, more worried than I thought I could be.

"Sorry Psyc, I didn't mean to throw it at you, my anger took over." Watching as my soulless dust begins to swallow his gold, coming off the tips of his wings; my panic for what I have done sets my heart pounding.

"You can..." A hiss stopping him mid-sentence "Fly?" He hisses again, my dust causing him pain.

"Yes, I can fly... something has changed with me" I say, stepping back from the fairy beloved by all.

"How?" He hisses again, the blackness nearly completing its journey of full domination.

"Well, it's a long story. But I'm not sure what I have done to you. This is all new"

"What do you mean? You threw your dust at me." He says clearer, standing to his feet, the black now coming off his wings just like mine. "And you've stolen my rods"

"Your rods? But… no, they're mine. I asked anyone if they were theirs and no one answered." I say defensively, knowing full well I'm in the wrong.

"Huh" He says.

"What? What's the matter with you?" I ask

"What's the matter with me, that's rich! Why is your dust black, why is my dust now black?" He panics, holding up his right hand as he forms a small pile of shine-less dust.

"I don't…"

"What? Know? Well, you shouldn't be throwing your dust at people. Especially new dust that you've never had before, what have you done to me?" His voice keeping at a nice level.

Annoying me with his easiness, I shrug my shoulder.

"That's it. That's all you going to give me?" Shaking his afro head of hair, he looks dumbstruck. "All I've ever done is be nice to you. When no one else would talk to you, I tried. When every fairy forgot about you, ignored your existence, I fought your corner. All I wanted was to be your friend, a real friend. Do you know why I dropped when you came up behind me?"

Shaking my head, I look at Psyc with fresh eyes. Even now with me turning his dust a death black, he still wants to be kind to me. He still wants to speak to me, to help me. Why. I was sure it was all an act, certain of it. Nerdiver had to be wrong about him. About this, he cannot care for me. Why would he, I'm the fairy without dust, a useless being. I couldn't even create children if I wanted to, but now. Could I have been wrong this whole time.

"I thought you were one of my stupid fans. Yes. I'm a good flyer, and a great fairy but I never asked to be. All this, I never asked for, I never asked for the other fairies to love me. They annoy me more than anything. No one wants to know me, all they want is to know the amazing Psyc!" He puffs, his wings seeming to bend on an angle, his gold disappearing fully. "Did you know that? Not the real me, the Psyc who creates things like a dwarf can, my dust is unique in a different way. Or it was" He hisses "It's different in a way no one wants to find out about. Flighty, fairies can do so much more than we think. If we could only try! Does anyone care though... no! But I thought... well maybe... you might have."

"Psyc..." I begin to say, wanting, in the first time I've ever really listened to him, to apologise for the way I've acted.

"No! You don't get to change tactics now. Look what you've done to me!" He holds out his hands, creating black dust that flows to the floor around him. "You've stolen from me!" He points at the rods "You've always been rude to me. And you have never! Ever shown any interest in finding out who I am!

He shouts, his own anger coming to the forefront, the darkness growing inside him.

"Psyc, I never thought you really wanted to be my friend. Me the dustless fairy..." I say trying my best to do the one thing I've never done before.

"Why do you think I always came alone! You idiot! We could have been friends... best friends... even..." Stopping himself, he glares at me before pain suddenly takes over body fully.

"Psyc" I scream, as a lion-like scream bursts from his lips.

Bending back, he screams as something inside rips to come out. Ripping at his soul, at the man I never let him give me the chance to show. Dust pouring out of his hands at an alarming rate, the space around us dies. Turning cold and dead from the dust flowing from him, the ground beneath us gives off the smell of rot.

Scared and unsure what to do, I move to touch him. My own dust begins to flow out of my palms taking control of me. Panicked, knowing I don't want to hurt him even more, I stop myself. Watching him on his back, convulsing in pain, from the jealousy I have wrought. Terror of the curse I have given him does its own will upon him, changing his screams, shifting them to shrieks, a dust battle happening inside.

What have I done. What is this elven blessing I have been cursed with. What is this plague of death I have brought to my home. To my forest. To Psyc. So many question's with no answers, my eyes start to water.

Tears breaking my eyes, I bounce backwards, fleeing the dying fairy. Like the coward I am, I fly away.

Leaving a trail of dust pouring out of my hands into the forest below, I let the disaster I have brought upon Psyc, poison the world around me.

The dust of death

Death everywhere I go, every place I hover or stop or cry. Yes, I said cry, how can this have happened. How could I ever think this soulless dust could be a blessing the forest needs. This is what I get, what I get for trying to find the missing part of me. The macho fairy with his big arms and wide chest; the naturally grown muscles shaped to the opposite to any other of my kind. The manly fairy that cannot fly nor have any dust, a male fairy that couldn't even be called a fairy. I am the one fairy that may have just killed the best of our race, I'm the one who left him to die alone. Is this the person I truly am?

Doing something so I was the forgettable fairy, testing myself further than I thought I could go, this is what I get. Dead trees rot up around me, my darkness breaking down the biggest of the forest's gems. All crumbling under the darkness I have let take over me, the darkness I am now, I feel always now, materializing out of my palms, crushing my soul.

Flying dead straight, I know I am aiming for the one place I shouldn't go near. To the one person, I don't want to hurt. The one person who may understand what is happening to me. The only place, I always feel safe and welcome no matter how or why I go there.

"Nerdiver!" I scream, hopping in my darkening heart that she can somehow hear the tiny voice of the fairy of death.

Whispering her name over in my mind, my vision blurs as I flap my wings harder than I think they can move. My dust sprinkling out my hands, I wonder how long it will be until I collapse, my dust draining me dry.

Trailing over my feet, I feel every drop escaping the base of my wings, filtering down to curse the bluebells running under me. Blackening the sunflowers to their roots, they try to continue standing tall in a gap of pine trees. Animals and insects alike try fleeing, feeling the wave of the fairy death coming in their direction.

Screaming, I shoulder an oak leaf out my way, bursting my death dust all over it. Running up its body, my dust turns the branch black, crawling up the whole ancient tree so it can consume it. My darkness taking over my trail I fly, I don't dare look behind me, not wanting to see the destruction and devastation I'm leaving in my wake.

Building dams solely by manual labour, I have made the forest bloom in a way that no other fairy has been able to do. All I wanted was the easy way, a natural way to be able to help any forest like any fairy. Instead, I'm killing it, turning this magical place into a world of shadow.

A cluster of silver birch trees, with millions of overhanging leaves, come before me. Screaming at my insides to stop the dust, I don't want to curse the white trunks into my darkness.

Pumping from my palms, I feel black seeping out of me. My wings just keeping me up, the dust seems to burn at my legs trailing behind me. Stretching in a horrible way, the skin on my hands feels like it is going to rip apart. My dust burning its way out of my body, ready to kill, even me.

Fluttering past everything, I hear the squeaks of a creature scurrying away from my path. Diving to the left and right, animals of all sizes, can see the shadow I'm bringing with me. Not wanting my darkness to touch its soul, the hedgehog with the Viking blue eyes looks me straight in the eye before scurrying away.

The darkness I feel biting at me from inside, calls out to the world around me, wanting to hurt anything it can. Just like how I've hurt Psyc, I beg that he's okay. True, I had pure anger pushing towards him, but I never wanted to curse him. I never wanted to change him, turn his brilliant golden dust into the death touch I am bringing on this world. Will he even be okay after I've shrouded him in my blackness, in this curse Master helped me attain or is he already long gone.

Forcing myself to think of Master, I remember how the rock troll said all he wanted to do was help me. Though, what can he gain from this death cursing through my body. What need does he have this curse for, he who is the reason I have it. The well is for blessings but mixed with the dark cup he created, its darkness swimming at the base. For all I know, it may have altered my rightful power.

Screaming out to my mermaid again, I beg for her to be waiting for me.

"Nerdiver tell me you hear me!" I scream, knowing for sure that I'm closer to her than I should be.

Blasted off course by a gust of wind, I spin in the air, my hands grabbing out at anything in reaching distance. Ripping off a flowers petal, I let myself spin; my eyes watching my touch turn the carnation into a shrivelled black mess.

Hitting my shoulder into a tree from behind, I cry out as my wing gives out. Sending me dropping to the floor like a rock thrown by a giant, I hit the ground like dead weight. Pain screaming out of me, my wings feel crushed, my back giving off an odd heat and my legs giving me nothing at all.

Have I just broken my whole body? Is this something that happens to a lot of fairies when they fly if they're not paying attention. I don't want to lie here cursing the forest until I die of hunger. This cannot be my destiny.

Lifting my hands, my back groans at me from the movement. My dust finally stopping for a moment, I feel a small sense of peace. Smiling at this small benefit, I lean my head to the left to scope out my surroundings.

Ferns hanging over me, they hide the rest of the forest from my view. The sun breaking through the tiny gaps between the ferns leaves; it makes them look like they have been cut with a pair of scissors with teeth broken into the blades.

Circling around my new broken body, the dirt here turns dark. My wings still giving off the dust of death, they seem to try and fix themselves under my heavy weight. Calling them to my body, I feel the soft brush as they wiggle into their rightful mould, mending back to their beautiful shape. With my head still to the left, I can see one of my top wings curl up over my shoulder, back under my clothing, my shirt ripped open from the spinning motion.

Cooling my back, the black outline of my wings, which they never had before the well, seems to begin to counteract the damaging heat running all over me. Feeling a flash from the centre of my back, the feeling in my legs returns instantly, allowing me to shake the darkness out of me.

My body feeling lighter, I push up onto my hands, giving my body the time it may need to feel better. Surprising myself entirely, I feel great. My wings want to de-attach from my body and flutter me to wherever I want to go.

Ignoring this impulse, I get to my feet and hold my hands in two balls. Getting to Nerdiver's pond without another infection to the forest is all I want. Walking may be the only way to make sure that doesn't happen, but can I stop these palms for releasing dust for long. I cannot be so sure.

Going on instinct, I know that the way to Nerdiver's will be the direction I choose with my soul. Pushing by the ferns, I walk right, and then circle around a huge broken oak tree. Split in two from what looks like a lightning strike, the time it takes me to circle the roots begins to bring me back to the world I was living only a few days before.

How can I have hated it so much, this life of having no need to rush anywhere. Be anywhere, I didn't want to be. To be able to have a fulfilling life blooming the forest in the way that nature wanted me to. Not in this dark way I have cursed myself and the rest of the forest with.

Making it to the other side of the tree, I take another look at my hands, keeping them closed, so I don't lose control. The curse I have brought on Psyc, the infection I left him to writhe within pain. Is this the fairy I always wanted to be, someone whose power leaches everything that is light in the world.

Maybe he did really want to be my friend like he said, or maybe he was just teasing me. Does that give me the right to hurt him like that. To kill him even. Like every plant or tree or flower I have passed today, I have changed them with my curse. If they survive and grow in the darkness, what will they become in the forest of life and beauty.

Most I know will have withered and died, this is the gift I have brought upon myself, on Psyc. His golden dust showing the light his body possessed; I feel in my bones, if anyone is not going to be able to accept this curse, it will be him.

Clocking the outer rocks, running around the familiar pond, I run at it. I run once again from Psyc and the death I may have caused him. The pain I felt he so rightly deserved for being kind to me. I, the fairy of darkness is once again, the only one of his kind.

With two tears released from my water ducts, I cannot help but let my sadness take over the only emotion I have been able to feel for years. My anger. Unpeeling my wings, I push off the ground leaving a trail of death behind me, aiming for one of my tunnels I knocked out alone, a set of stairs that head straight to my true friend.

Being the coward I am, I hide at the centre of the tunnel. Legs drawn up into my chest, I let the sadness consume me, my pain at what I am taking over. Nerdiver will come and when she does she will call me to her.

Whimpering her name one last time, as I sit halfway up the tallest set of stairs I have built into the rocks surrounding her pond. I let my voice echo up to the still water, sending my pain to the mermaid of the pond.

"Nerdiver..."

A promise made

"Little Bug?"

Snapping my head up, I let my tears continue to fall, recognising that saying instantly. Why is Master appearing now? After he left me to deal with this all on my own.

"Come out little bug. I wish to speak to you" His scraping voice, scratches up the tunnel to me. How does he even know I'm here?

"Little bug, I don't like to be kept waiting. I've come here to see you, the least you could do is let me see my friend." Filling me with guilt, I realise he may not even know what has happened to me. For all he knows it worked, and I have my lilac dust and my fairy magic is ready to pollinate the forest.

Crawling to my feet, I decide to head up the stairs. Moving towards Nerdiver's pond is the better option, a better option to stand my ground against my known caller. Knowing Nerdiver may take a whole day before she comes to my call, I know she will come eventually. If Master isn't the friend he pretends to be, he will have a shock of his own at her presence.

Walking out into the open air, I stand on top of the rock I cracked in two. Hiding from me only days before, Master re-appears from behind the rock, the stone beneath me being the same height as him. Unlike the well, I have the upper hand of being above him this time.

Wiping my face quickly, I hide the fact that I've been crying. I don't want to see the reaction this rock troll will give me at the sight of my sadness. Smiling his wide mouth just like before, I see the orchids that appear over his body at different points have changed colour. Changed to black. Matching the colour of my dust, I can't help but wonder if he has control over the colour they give off.

"Why are you hiding in the tunnel alone? I would have thought you would be flying all over this forest. Up and over the tree line even?" He asks, sounding genuinely surprised at me.

"Well... I just wanted some alone time" I say, still not certain if I want to tell him what has happened to me.

"But you've been blessed! Everything you've ever wanted, ever deserved! Flighty my dear fairy, you should be out there spreading your dust, darkening the forest before everyone's eyes!" He beams, his words not sinking in straight away.

"How would you know my dust even came to me?" I ask

"I was there-" Cutting him off I suddenly realise he said spreading darkness. He knows the curse that has become of me.

"Wait!" I scream "You know my dust is death. You know the curse that has become of me, rather than the blessing I was promised"

"Promised? Little bug, there was never any promise given to you. The well gives what it deems is rightful, true to the being brave enough to drink from its well."

"Rightful? The well thinks I deserve the touch of death. How is that possible, there has to be some mistake?" I question the well, not aiming it at Master "But Nerdiver said the well blesses the drinker or kills them. She never said anything about an alternative. Unless... unless it was you!" I shout, pointing at the rock troll, the only other creature there that could have altered the blessing. "You gave me a cup; you created one from your own magic. Rock troll magic... magic I know nothing of or its consequences!"

"Now calm down Flighty, you have no knowledge of my magic, it is no concern of yours" The rock trolls voice turns harsh.

"I thought I saw something dark at the base of the cup, something wanting to come to me. You cursed it. So, in turn, you cursed my blessing, cursed the elven water and cursed me!" I shout, feeling my dust coming forth.

"I have told you already little bug calm down. If you calm yourself I can explain" The troll's voice becomes calm again.

Calming myself to the best of my ability, this beast has cursed me. Turned me into a creature I was never meant to be, wanted to be. I could have had my beautiful dust if I had only drunk the water before he came. If I had only walked away when he had appeared, none of this would have happened.

The forest would have been fine and I would not have hurt Psyc.

"It's your fault I have killed the forest, it's your fault I hurt Psyc!" I scream, my pain and anger coming out through tears. Listening to my emotions, my dust sprinkles out of my hands flowing over the stones smooth skin below me, trailing into the still water.

"The forest is only partly dead. The points you have dusted have either withered or bloomed. Grown into something new, into the power we need for the fight for this magical forest. You have bloomed nature into something deserving against the tyranny of the elven race." Moving closer to my rock, Master places his hands on either side of me just like he did at the well.

"Something deserving-" I begin to counter but he stops me.

One hand in the air, he motions for me to be quiet. It is his time to talk, to teach. In his mind, the kind race that has never treated my race wrongly needs to be overthrown. Apart from the cruelness of trapping Nerdiver in her pond world, Elves have never done anything of note, of a tyrant in my eyes. But closing my mouth, I sit on the rock as I let my dust continue to crawl out of my palms, becoming my shield of darkness, protecting me from this brute.

Noticing from the way he places his hands on the rock, Master does not wish to touch my dust. The upper hand I have never felt I've had, swims inside me like a fuel, filling on arrogance I always felt Psyc was only able to possess.

"Where to begin… well Flighty, do you remember we had a deal? I help you drink from the well of blessing and you help me when I come calling?" He asks, looking straight into my eyes, knowing that I could never forget the deal he has cursed me with.

"This is not me calling you on our deal. I wish to see the power I have helped you gain, to ask you to first join me. But I'm also here to give a friendly reminder that when my favour comes up, you have no choice but to oblige. If you join me, however, the need for your favour in return may never come to pass. So what do you say?"

"What are you asking me to join exactly?"

"The fight of course!" He shouts spreading his arms wide, like I'm meant to know just what he's on about.

"The fight for what?"

"The forest!" He shouts once again.

"Is that why you cursed me?" I ask, confused why my death dust is needed. Surely if Master wins the forest, he would want it to be healthy, not dead or cursed. This curse he has given me cannot be just for this, just to kill or change the forest for the worse. Bringing me back to our conversation

Master brings me closer to him, touching my dust without any worry.

"No that is not the reason I have done this to you" Surprised that he seemed so cautious of my dust at first, my magic just moves over his stone hands just like the rock that's under me.

Brought forward to his face, I now sit right in front of his huge round nose. Smoother than my hair still pulled up in a top knot, his nose is the only comfortable part of this magical creature. Looking up into his right eye, the soulless dark colour matching my dust. Asking why he did this to me, I hold up my hands above my head showing my dust as it still pours free.

"I have done this for Nimfa" He says, thinking I will know who that is.

"Who is Nimfa?" I ask, the answer hitting me straight away. "The only female rock troll left?"

"Correct... there are only ten in the whole of this forest. One female and nine males. Four are in love with each other, but unlike your race, we cannot produce more of our kind with the same sex. That leaves..."

"Five... there's five rock trolls all trying to fight for her affection. But if you need to repopulate your race, wouldn't it be easier for her to have children with all of you. Like bees do, she will be your queen?" I ask the obvious question to me.

"No" He huffs

"Why because of your pride? This is your race we are talking about" I ask confused how on the brink of extinction he can be so foolish.

"Only one can breed with her. Like you said she's our queen. She's our true queen, and when her children grow, others will be needed to breed with her offspring. And their offspring, you see rock trolls can live for a very long time, so every generation needs to get new bloodlines into them so crossbreeding doesn't happen. At least until there is enough of my kind again." He explains to me, making a very good point.

"So you need me why? To overthrow the Elves. Is this an important need when there is so few left of your race?"

"Nimfa will only breed with the bravest and strongest of our kind. She is the Queen and her first in line with follow in that power. She will only have the best!" He shouts, raising his chest in the air. "I am the best… but to prove it I need to win her the forest. Her kingdom!"

"I don't know if I can help you" I say quietly

"Why not?" He sneers leaning right in.

"I cannot control this... power. I will be a hindrance. Do you truly want to give your queen, a kingdom full of death and darkness? The magic you have, it is not meant for this. No one wants to bring their children into a home of death; they want the world to be bright and beautiful. A world that they can live a happy existence. That is all I ever wanted."

"Rubbish! You wanted power, you wanted revenge. I saw that you attacked that other fairy, I have seen the way you took those diamonds. I have watched you every step of the way to get to this point. If you will not join me, you will do my bidding when I ask for the favour you promised me. Trust me little bug, it is better to be on my side than against me." Master warns, his voice growing with anger "I will be the ruler of this forest, stood next to my queen. I wish for you to be on my shoulder for the next phase of my life, for the time I will grow this world into the palace it needs to be."

"The pain I have put Psyc through... you saw him. Wait you saw him!" I panic hoping that he's okay "You were there when I fled. Is he okay? Is he alive?"

"Your fairy enemy is no concern now. Listen to me little bug, you have faced your enemy and won. After all this is done, after all this fighting is finished and my queen is ruler, I swear I will help you find a way to become the light fairy you wish to be. But I need you now. I need you to be the darkest fairy this forest will ever know. The fairy of death is the fairy I must have by my side... Are you him?"

A light fairy. Is that what he can promise. He lied to me once at the well, will he not just lie to me again now. Get me to do anything he wishes, so he can rule, so I can be his weapon. The first fairy to ever spread a rock troll's evil, spread his darkness to every point of this lush green forest. For what, for some magic that I may finally be owned at the end. A little bit of light magic which I can use to heal the forest if we can find a cure.

"I will only join you if you promise on the life of the children I help you bring to this world, that you will help me find a way to bring light back to the darkness I create?"

Nodding, I give him a hard stare showing that a nod is not enough of a promise.

"Yes, I promise I will help you find a cure, on the lives of my children I have with Nimfa one day" Scraping his index finger over his heart, the familiar spark comes to life as he carves a circle on his left chest. Giving off a small glow, the moment he takes his finger away, I feel a burning on my chest, like he is doing the same to me in this moment.

Ripping my shirt apart, I feel a scar scrapping into my soft skin. Watching with wide eyes, I see the glowing circle to match my new friends, is glowing with the same fire that sparked down his forearm when he created my dark cup.

"I will return to you soon, but I have many things to prepare. Tell no one of our plan or the promise I have given you little bug" Dipping his head, Master looks at me dead in the eye waiting for my own promise to him.

"I promise"

"Stop this!" Nerdiver's scream shakes the rock I am standing upon.

Turning around I see Nerdiver flying up into the air, aiming a globe of water in her hands at Master's face. Gleaming in the sunlight, her snake green skin counters the ball of blue she has in her left palm, letting it free as she comes towards me.

Landing on the rock next to me hard, she screams so high and loud, I cannot help but cover my ears. Dropping onto all fours, my ears feel as though they are splitting, ripping down to their cores. Using all her defence techniques, Nerdiver aims her scream at Master, followed by another globe of water.

Forcing myself to push through her power, I look up at Master, surprised that he's frozen in place. Looking at me as one more globe of water hits him, he mouths "I will return for you my death" before sinking into the ground at his feet, a look of pure pain on his face.

Overcome with her scream, my mind cannot take the pain any longer. With darkness raining down upon my vision, it drags me into the heart of my power.

A true friend's gift

"Wake, Flighty Wake up"

Coaxed out of my darkness, I hear her voice singing to me.

"Flighty he's gone, I need you to wake up" Opening my eyes, all I can see is the blue sky above. Passed out on my back, the soft rock beneath me seems to keep me cool from the sun directly in the centre of the tree circle.

"Look at me Flighty. Are you feeling alright? It's me, Nerdiver" Saying her name like I don't know who she is, her usually powerful voice doesn't seem to affect me the same way as usual.

With a ringing still in my ears, I joke with her. "Can you stop that screaming now; it's still going through me"

"No. Oh no what have I done, Flighty I'm so sorry, I only meant to aim it at him." Hovering over me, she blocks out the view of the sky above, the dread that she's broken me is written all over her midnight eyes.

Smiling, I see her silky skin is drier than usual from hovering above the water. Webbed fingers covering her mouth, the shock of what she's done, looks down at me. Seeing my face she backs off, a little hurt at my jokiness.

"I'm okay, I was only kidding. I have a little ringing in my ear, but I assume that will go away. Funny thing though Nerv, your voice isn't doing its usual magic on me" Smiling at her, I feel happy that for the first time ever, I don't have to fight her voice but can truly just listen to her.

"Oh Flighty, that's because I used my cruel scream. It is meant to kill a hunter or attacker, if I had aimed it at you, you would not be here right now. Though maybe it has instead broken the magical pull my voice has had over you all these years." Smiling herself, her sharp teeth gleams at me as if I were prey.

Use to this smile, if she wasn't my true friend I may run in fear. Doing the opposite, I pull myself to my feet and look at her. The girl who is trapped here, stuck in this pond for as long as she will live. If only I hadn't listened to that Rock troll, I could be breaking her free of this cage.

"Nerdiver, the blessing... it has gone so terribly wrong." I say, breaking down again now that my friend is here to catch my pain.

"I know... I have seen the dust sprinkling down as I rose to you. I came as fast as I could. The moment your voice touched my soul, I swam to you" And by soul, she means her ear holes. Swimming closer to me, I scurry away; afraid I will hurt her like I have hurt Psyc.

"Tell me what has happened, but do not be afraid, your dust does not affect the world under the ocean, so in turn, it does not affect me." In show of the truth, Nerdiver quickly dives under the water to return to the top with a hand full of my black dust.

"But how? My new dust destroys and is holy death. How can it not affect your world?" I quiz, my mind confused, knowing I will never see the world she has come from.

"My world is alive and thrives on different aspects to the world outside of the water. Where you see green, I see blue. Where trees grow tall up here, reefs grow out, taking over the land wide, rather than in height. Height is not needed in the world I come from, as the water and sea are free to have as much open space as they need. If only I could show you my world Flighty." With wonder in her voice, she looks as if she may disappear underwater again so I snag her with my story.

"Nerdiver, my journey was as you said. I had to climb high, higher than I have ever gone, to nearly be eaten by the bird of prey who has hunted me all these months."

"No!" Nerdiver says shocked, surprised to this day why that bird has such an aim for my little person.

"Yes, but I buried myself in the lands, hiding myself from its evil intent. I then had to journey across a stream, but the current was too strong and I was nearly washed away. These tests whatever they are, are clearly only made for me. Any other fairy would have been fine. Where did you hear of them?" I ask, still curious to how she finds out all the information she is given at this lonely pond. Is there a secret she has been keeping from me since we were both younglings?

"Tell me the rest of your story first; I want to know how this has all gone terribly wrong." Motioning for me to continue, I explained how I made it to the well, with the elf frozen as a statue in death. I tell her of the diamond knife and the passion behind the unknown killer. I say how I had changed my mind, how the risk I felt wasn't worth the pain of never getting to see her again, or live the life I was clearly given.

Proud of me, Nerdiver still couldn't understand how I went from making my mind up and kicking my cup in the well to having darkness flowing through me.

"How did this become your blessing? This does not seem like a blessing to me. From the pain I feel from your voice to the blackness of your eyes. Your beautiful lilac colouring has vanished. Your eyes are as black as mine."

"Master" I say through gritted teeth, knowing he will return for me. With the promise burning on my chest, the rock troll will return to use me, take me until I help him with his fight. Knowing this, I know I can only tell Nerdiver half the truth, half of what has happened. Psyc I can explain, the sorrow I feel at being a coward. At being too afraid to return to see if he has survived, if he has become more powerful because of my curse. I will only tell Nerdiver everything that has happened up until I came to cry under the rocks I stand upon today.

"Master?" She asks

"Master was the rock troll you have beaten away."

"Oh, that round ball of stone. I have met only one other, but it was very different." She says, averting her gaze from me.

"Nerdiver, I am no fool"

"What?" She says, looking scared that her secret has come out.

"I know you must have other visitors from time to time. You're a one in a million kind of creature, with a pure heart and sound advice. I am not jealous of these friends of yours. But you are my best friend no?" I ask a little hope that the others are not true friends.

"Of course you are my only best friend, but pure heart I cannot agree with."

"It is not for you to agree upon, it is a fact. Now, are you ready to hear the part of how this" I say holding out my hands at my sides, letting my dust pour out "Happened to me?"

Nodding, she leans back into the water, with only her shoulder not covered up, the smooth texture of the liquid, looks so inviting.

Talking slowly so I do not get ahead of myself, I tell her all that has transpired. Starting with Master's appearance out of nowhere to the conversation we had. I tell her everything we said, or as close to what I could remember. I explain the magic I never knew they possessed. Not surprising, she agrees she knew nothing of their magic until her visit from one herself.

"What did the Rock troll that visited you, show you? Did they perform magic for you?" I ask, genuinely interested.

"Again Flighty, for another time. All I can say is that it was not this Master that you are referring too." Staring at me hard, I can tell she wants to know the full story before she tries and works out a way to help me. That is the one thing I can always count on from Nerdiver; she will help me whenever she can, if it is within her power.

Finishing in a blur of an explanation, I tell her everything that happened after I drank from the cup. Everything that has brought me to this point, even ruining the surprise of the diamonds I have collected for her. Telling her in tears, I explain the actions I choose, by accident or on purpose to inflict on Psyc.

Back on my bum, I cry at the death that has become of me. The power that has taken its toll, even in the few days it's been a part of me. Giving me one quick look, Nerdiver dives down into her pond, leaving me alone once again. Clearly, my actions and the curse I am is something she cannot be around, I wipe my wet face. Even my best friend, my soul buddy cannot be around me.

Getting back to my feet, I blink my eyes, while unpeeling my wings. Shaking myself, I know they only thing I can do is wait for Master to come find me. In the meantime, I might as well learn to control these dreadful powers.

Kicking off from the ground, I push up into the air, feeling the way the air wraps itself around my membrane wings. The part of me that always wanted to be used, until I choose to take what was never meant to be mine.

"Flighty. Stop, come down here." Nerdiver's voice flies up to me "I am only going away for a moment, but I will return. What you have said does not scare me. You are my friend and I will help you."

Dropping back down to the rock, she gives me a smile. "Stop being dramatic"

Diving back in, I huff at her statement of me being dramatic. What a thing to say, is all I can think as I peel my wings back to my skin and lie down onto my pile of black dust.

With time flying by, I cannot help thinking she may not truly return. The sun now gone behind the circle of trees, I wait, wondering if my hunger will vanish like she has.

Re-emerging, Nerdiver's bald head lets the water run down her face, rolling over her shoulders as she pushes herself up. If I hadn't known her since I was a youngling, her naked humanoid upper half would embarrass me from staring. Though even a creature as small as me can appreciate the body of a beautiful woman. Tail doing all the work; she does not speak to me but looks directly at my waistline. Confused I look down myself to see Psyc black velvet bag, still hanging there after all that has happened to me. Waiting patiently for me to have the courage to touch it, the golden strings reminds me of the fairy I may have killed once again.

"Why are you looking at this? I forgot I had it if I'm honest." I say, undoing the string holding it to my body.

"Do you trust me fully?" She asks, swimming closer to me in a slow movement.

"Of course I do, but I don't want to hurt you" I step back, making it clear that I'm not comfortable with her touching me. I know she has held my black dust, but what if it hurts her when it hasn't been in the water first.

"You cannot hurt me. I am the one that has hurt you" Lifting her arms out to me as she bridges the gap between us, she gives me a sad look.

"Stop Nerdiver!" I shout making her pause "We don't know what this dust can truly do"

"Flighty, it is my fault this has happened to you. I was the one who told you about the well of blessings. I was the one who filled your head with the idea of gaining the power you have always felt the need to have. So now... I am the one who is going to help you change for the better" Singing her last words, she takes me in her right hand.

"Put the dust in my left hand, but be sure not to touch it" She warns, making it clear that this is key for whatever she is about to do.

Opening the top of the velvet bag, Psyc golden dust glows out of it, lighting my face in the setting sun. Pouring it out, I fill the small space in Nerdiver's hand, watching as the dust seems to warm her. A shiver running through her, she tells me she has to do this quickly or the dust may change her instead.

Confused, I do not understand what she means; knowing better than her that fairy dust cannot change creatures. It has a few uses but it is limited in the outcomes it can manage. It is not like rare elven magic that is only seen every few generations. Elves do not have children very often, with the length of time their lives go on for, and power is only given to the best of light and dark.

Humming a tune that is made up of long beats, Nerdiver submerges me into the water, pulling my body under without any warning. Unable to take in a breath; I pull a large amount of water in as she pushes her left hand tight around me, already grasped in her right.

Crying out, I never thought Nerdiver would kill me. Her only plan was to drown me in her pond, the place I gave myself the goal of breaking her out of. Choking on the water filling up my lungs, I cannot even scream, the water taking over my whole body.

Closed within my friend's huge hands, I feel the heat of her, clutching me close, her silky skin holding me as tight as a python. Screaming my thoughts at her, I ask her why she is doing this. My body starting to jerk, the water taking its toll in a slow painful way, a death I could never have seen coming.

My body working on instinct, I try to take in one last breath, and to my surprise, it works. Either through imagination or a dream, I assume I must be dead. Feeling the water fill my lungs, filling me up like a glass, I know this can't be real. Breathing still, I cannot see or get my head around the fact that air seems to be keeping me alive.

Hands unclasping, Nerdiver lets me go, her work on my body complete. Swimming an inch away from me, Nerdiver lights up my darkened surroundings she's brought me to. Glowing white, long flowing locks circles her whole being. Coming out of the head I've only ever seen bald, I laugh stunned by her absolute beauty.

Certain she was beautiful before, the way she is underwater is a thousand times more magical. Curling down, her hair flows to about waist height, kissing the glowing river lines, running over her shoulders and arms. Moving down her sides and collar bones, the glowing lines on her, run all the way to her tail. A sea creature of legend, her light brightens the darkness all around.

Never viewing her as ugly, Nerdiver has just become the most beautiful creature I have ever seen. Forgetting the fact that I am somehow alive under water, I smile at her, wishing I could speak to her.

You are breath-taking Nerv, if only I could tell you this. I think at her, wondering if we rise back up I can tell her. About to nod in an upward direction, I'm taken underwater more, her voice in my mind.

You just did. And thank you Flighty, this is something I have always thought about you. With your new golden glow, you help light up my little world of darkness.

How have I just heard her voice? How am I breathing right now? What does she mean by me glowing gold? Confusion running all over my mind, she tilts her head at me. Thinking at her, I look down to see a trail of dust sprinkling over my feet. A mix of gold and black, it pours out of my wings, lighting the space up around me even more.

You now have one eye glowing gold and one black. She smiles thinking into my mind. *When I doused you in Psyc's dust, its blended into you, giving you the gift I wanted it to. The gift to be able to breath underwater like me. You now have gills, you're part sea creature. With the mix of his dust and gift given to you, your wings are now veined with both black and gold. Your lilac, however, I am not sure, will ever come back. But I have a feeling your fairy magic will open up to you more than any other fairy now. You have a touch of darkness and light in you Flighty.* Her sweet voice singing at me, it fills my head with too much information.

The silliest thing is, the first piece of information I latch onto is that I will never get to see the lilac glow in my hands. The colour she always said my eyes turn when I was angry, I only saw flashes of it reflected in my wings from time to time. Changing me this way doesn't seem possible; fairy magic doesn't warp reality or a creature's biology. It is for blooming and growing the forest. *How did this work, tell me how you knew you could do this. Tell why you knew of the well of blessing.*

Flighty... She thinks, swimming around me.

Using my wings with my second load of dust flowing through me, I push myself just like when I fly, spinning in the water following my talented friend. Joining or saving her was all I ever planned to do and now I'm here.

Seeing the huge space she has had to swim around in, it feels humongous for me. Watching the beauty she possesses when out of the air, I understand the beauty she has always craved to have when above the waterline. Will I ever be able to live above the waterline again. How will I ever complete my promise to Master burned into my skin.

Scaring me over the chest with a simple flare of heat, I know the circle is a reminder to me of the pact we have. How he will come down to get me I am not sure, but exploring this world, my new world. With Nerdiver it's something I'm ready for and gaining the answers she's been hiding from me is my first priority. Master will return when he is ready and hopefully I will be too.

Are you ready to explore? Are you ready for the new phase in your life? The world under the waterline? Thinking this at me while I swim down in the depths of the darkness below, her voice is a much-needed comfort in this new time.

Looking up, I can see Nerdiver has brought me down quite a way. With the sunlight lighting up half of the walls to me, I bath in the last of the light before turning to my mermaid lighting our new direction. Below me, Nerdiver is truly bright, luring me into the unknown places full of secrets I must have.

Flapping my new golden, black tinged wings, I spin in the water once and aim for where Nerdiver has disappeared into. Setting off like a rocket, I push myself through my new home, the water rushing in through my mouth and into my lungs, my new gills taking out all the oxygen I need from the water. Swimming through all the air bubbles waiting for me to take in the as much O2 as I want, I absorb all I need, pushing my wings behind me hard, propelling me into the ponds calm embrace.

This world will continue in...

Nerdiver

Enjoyed Flighty?

Leave a review Online

Follow **HDA Pratt**
On Instagram **@hdapratt** or
Follow the **HDA Pratt author page** on facebook.
Keep up to date with all of HDA's latest news on his website

hdapratt123.wixsite.com/hdapratt

Book two of A Magical Creature series

Is walking away from your sworn duty the only way to be
happy?
Releasing a cursed friend from a life of destruction, a mermaid's
binding helpfulness may only be the beginning...
Can an attack to her home bring with it the fate of her whole
world...

Nerdiver

Available in paperback or Ebook on amazon today!

Other series by HDA Pratt

Even immortals can be hunted...
Even immortals can feel fear...
For one Night Creature, a sleepless time may about to begin.

The Sleepless Night Creature

Printed in Poland
by Amazon Fulfillment
Poland Sp. z o.o., Wrocław

64345303R00070